I0710016
Rebel
Desire
a romantic comedy
LK FARLOW

PROLOGUE - COLTON

"No!" I tell the purple-haired menace darkening the doorway of my office. "Absolutely not."

"But you don't even know why I'm here!" She stomps her foot, like a petulant child at the start of a temper tantrum. In fact, I've seen my godchild do this very thing, and he's two.

"And I don't care, either. Leave," I reiterate, refusing to let my temper get the better of me. This woman punches every single one of my buttons, and something tells me the notion would delight her—which is un-fuck-ing-acceptable.

"Colt—Mr. Banks—please. Five minutes. No, four! Just give me four minutes, surely you can spare me that."

I bite my tongue, half tempted to tell her those two-hundred-and-forty seconds of my time equates to twenty dollars. "Make it two."

She nods, wisps of her oddly-colored locks escaping her ponytail with the motion.

"Your time starts now, Miss Murphy."

"Right! A bride is threatening to sue me! I didn't want to work with her to start with. She gave me bad vibes, and them together...let's just say they're not built to last. But she was persistent, and eventually, I relented, and she signed the contract and paid the deposit for the deluxe wedding package on the spot. But, on the day of her bridal pics—which we were doing at my studio—it was raining. *Talk about a bad omen,* right?" A full-body shiver works its way through her. "Anyway, I tried rescheduling because I don't use artificial lighting. It is *so* not my style. The clouds were completely covering the sun, so it was super doom and gloom. But she refused and demanded we do them anyway."

Ashley sucks in a deep breath before continuing.

"She wasn't happy with the pictures. She said they were too dark—well, no shit, Karen, it was practically pitch-black outside—and here's the kicker, I've already shot her wedding, and now she's refusing to pay the rest of her fee. So, obviously, I'm not giving her any pictures. And now she's threatening to sue me and is dragging me through the mud on social media!"

Once her rant is finished, all I can do is stare, in utter shock. *Who knew you could fit so many fucking words into one-hundred-and-twenty seconds?*

She must take my silence as an invitation to keep talking. Because sure enough, her lips are moving. Again. "Stacia said you were the best and so, help?" She wrings her hands and licks her lips. "Please?"

That single word tacked onto the end of her monologue almost breaks me; the way her voice pitched an octave higher with it, her lower lip wobbling, almost had me agreeing to take her on. Luckily, common sense prevailed. Ashley Murphy, while delectably hot, is a headache I neither want nor need.

I suck in a breath through my teeth, bowing my head a smidge. "Ah, sorry. No can do." I brush past her to open the door, ignoring the way her cinnamon-sugar scent tickles my nose. "I'd like to say it was nice seeing you, but, frankly, it wasn't. Let's not do this again anytime soon. Best of luck to you, Miss Murphy."

She flinches back, the movement almost imperceptible, even as her eyes glisten with unshed tears. I'll never know if Ashley let those tears fall, though, because she rolls her shoulders back and steps out onto the sidewalk with her head held high. "I'm not giving up!" she shouts as I shove the door closed in her wake, wishing like hell she would—give up, that is.

Two hours later, I'm still agitated. Ashley coming here without an appointment only reinforces everything I know about her. She's thoughtless, flighty, selfish, and unprofessional; it's no wonder someone is suing her.

I try and force myself to focus on the task at hand—research for a client—but I can't focus. Much to my displeasure, the look on Ashley's face right before she stormed out keeps torturing me, along with a plethora of unanswered questions.

Did she cry on the way to her car? Did she do a poor job on the client's pictures? Or is she the victim of a bridezilla?

It feels as if the walls of my spacious office are closing in on me. "Fuck!" I shove my chair back from my desk, snatching my phone as I stand. I dial up West. " 'Sup, man?" he asks, answering on the second ring.

"Headed out. Wanna grab dinner?"

"Depends; does your restaurant of choice have high chairs?"

I snort out a laugh. I can honestly say I never pictured West as a dad, but he's a fucking natural. Then again, Asher is a pint-sized badass. "I didn't have anywhere in mind. Hell, let him pick."

Now it's West who is laughing. "Hope you're ready for somewhere that offers toys with their kids' meals."

"I'm ready for anything that isn't this office."

"What's wrong?" he asks.

"Let's talk at dinner." We end our call with plans to meet up in thirty minutes—just enough time for me to run home and ditch the suit.

Twenty minutes later, I'm nursing a beer at a corner table of our favorite pizza place. My godchild has good taste—far better than any other snot-nosed kid I've ever met.

"Unca Tolton!" is all I hear before my godson launches himself at me, nearly tipping my chair with the force of his greeting.

"Ash-man!" I lift him onto my lap and offer him my hand for a high-five. I only cringe a little when his sticky fingers touch mine. Once he's situated in his own seat, I discreetly reach into my pocket for my hand sanitizer. *I love the kid, but he's a little germ bucket.*

"What's got your panties in a bunch?" West asks, plopping down into the seat beside his son.

"Panties are for girls," Asher says, not missing a beat as he arranges sugar packets on the table.

I cough to cover my laugh. "Your wedding photographer."

West raises a brow. "Ashley?"

"Obviously. Please catch up."

My friend opens his mouth to undoubtedly toss some smartass remark my way, but thinks better of it at the last minute. Like a naughty parrot, Asher has a tendency to repeat everything he hears—typically at the most inopportune time—so now everyone censors themselves in his presence.

Personally, I think it's hilarious. His parents…not so much. There's something about a toddler shouting *"What the fuck?"* at the top of his lungs on the play-ground after landing in a puddle at the bottom of the slide.

West regards me over the edge of his menu. "I'm gonna need an explanation here, man."

I drag my fingers through my hair. "She's crazy."

"Dat's not a nice word, Tolt."

West smirks at my being scolded by his toddler. "Sorry, little man," I say, offering him a fist bump, which he happily returns before diverting his attention back to his sugar packets.

"Good evening, boys," comes a soft, sensual voice from behind us. "I'm Darla, and I'll be your server tonight. Y'all ready to order?"

We quickly place our order, and my eyes follow Darla as she walks away, her long, red ponytail swinging and curvy ass bouncing with every step.

West snaps his fingers in front of my face. "Details, Colton, I want details."

"Where do I even start? She has to be the most unprofessional woman I've ever met."

West furrows his brow. "Unprofessional how? The previews we've seen of our photos are great. Stacia loves her."

"Did you know she hit on me at your wedding?"

"I'm sorry, she what?"

"Hit on me."

"Shit," West mutters.

Asher reaches over and tugs on West's shirt sleeve. "Bad word, Daddy."

"How? What did she say?"

I can't decide if he's asking because he's as appalled as I was or if he's winding me up. "She spent all night making eyes at me. And when she introduced herself, she placed her hand on my lapel."

West's eyes widen. "She didn't!"

I nod. "She did. Rubbed the fabric between her thumb and index finger, too."

"You're a"—he pauses to cover his son's ears—"a fucking idiot."

His hands fall back to his lap as I ask, "How so?"

"When an attractive woman shows interest in you, one of two things need to happen." He holds up his index finger. "One: if you're interested as well, you chat her up, maybe ask for her number." He adds another finger. "Two: if you're not into her, you let her down gently and move on. You don't stew on it for a week like a crazy person."

Winding me up, then. Got it. "It's not that she hit on me; I'm not a teenaged boy."

"Could've fooled me," my soon-to-be ex-best friend mumbles.

"As I was saying, it's not that she hit on me—even though doing so while working was *highly* unprofessional—she also showed up at my office this morning, demanding I offer her my legal counsel. Who does that?

Who barges into a professional setting, with no appointment, and starts making demands?"

"You're telling me her only crime is being unprofessional?" he asks, steepling his fingers beneath his chin.

I roll my eyes.

"And you don't find her attractive? At all?"

"What's that have to do with anything?" If I'm being truthful, she's not my type at all. I like my women petite, with lush curves, and Ashley's all long, straight lines. Hell, she's nearly as tall as I am.

West laughs. "You're clueless, man. Totally clueless."

CHAPTER 1
ASHLEY

have a sixth sense when it comes to love; I always have. It's like how some people can see ghosts, only I can see relationships. Not only can I sense when two people would be a good match, I can also tell if a relationship will stand the test of time.

Sounds crazy, I know, but it's true.

This ability of mine is part of why I love wedding photography. I only book couples who give me forever vibes—well, except that one time, but I'm hoping for the best. It's *such* an honor, knowing I'll be the one capturing the start of their lives together, immortalizing the moment they become one.

The downside to this whole shebang is I know exactly what kind of man I'll end up with. Well, not *exactly*-exactly. More of a broad stroke. A type, so to speak: sandy blond hair, blue eyes, a sharp jaw, and an even sharper tongue. Over the years, I've dated many men who fit the profile—and a few who didn't—in an effort to find him.

Fruitlessly, I might add. So, imagine my surprise

when I see *him*. One glance and my heart is racing, my palms sweating, and my belly feels like it's turned into a damn butterfly garden. Sure, these feelings are fairly normal for me when I'm working, but it's usually because I'm attuned to what my bride and groom are feeling.

But this time, it's the best man that has me reeling.

Simply put, he's gorgeous. My eyes trail over him for the umpteenth time, drinking in his delicious height. With me standing at five-nine, very few men make me feel small, but him…he has at least five inches on me. My mystery man has broad shoulders—the kind you want to sink your nails into while he pounds into you—and a trim waist. His dirty blond hair is the perfect length to run my fingers through, and his jaw looks as if it were carved from granite.

What really does me in, though, is his laugh: it's deep and hearty, and the way his Adam's apple bobs has me discreetly rubbing my thighs together.

I raise my camera and snap a few shots of him, along with the groom and another groomsman as they stand near the altar, waiting on the officiant to kick things off. Watching the three men interact fascinates me; my mystery man seems so comfortable, relaxed even, standing up there in front of everyone.

Surreptitiously, I capture a few more images of him, wanting to forever remember the way he runs the pad of his thumb over his lower lip.

Music fills the room, snapping me back into professional mode. With my camera poised and ready, I set to work capturing the first official day of West and his bride's forever.

I click away, capturing the bride's grandparents

escorting her mother down the aisle, followed by the bridal party: a tatted-up, green-haired knockout I know is married to the groomsman, and a curvy Penelope Garcia lookalike. Both women are working the white dresses they're wearing, but they pale in comparison to the bride.

Stacia looks like a vixen set on matrimonial bliss. Her black lace dress clings to every curve and show-cases the inked canvas of her skin to perfection. Her atomic red hair is piled atop her head, tendrils framing her face, and her lips are stained a deep crimson. She looks like a dark angel as she walks the aisle, escorted by her father on one side and her two-year-old son on the other.

The thought of editing these images has me giddy. The way West's eyes lit with pure joy at the sight of her, the way he kissed her with a passion that begged for privacy, without a single fuck given; the way their son covered his eyes and giggled. All of it, every single part of this wedding, has been pure perfection, and I know the reception will be as well.

And, if a certain hunky best man happens to talk to me…all the better.

I move toward the back of the ceremony space as the wedding party begins its trek back down the aisle. Warm fuzzies swirl within me as the love between Stacia and West lights up the room.

Feeling emboldened by all of the romance blanketing the room, I shoot my mystery man a flirty wink, hoping like crazy he'll approach me at some point during the reception.

He slows as he nears me, and my heart hiccups in my chest. *This is it! My one is going to talk to me!* I'm a jittery mess as he approaches. I wonder if he feels it, too—that we're meant to be.

He stops directly in front of me, holding up the entire processional. He leans in and—*oh my glob, he smells so good*—I freeze. "Hi," I whisper, feeling dazed. *Is he going to*—my thoughts get cut off when his breath tickles the shell of my ear.

"Did you even capture their first kiss?" he asks, his voice hard.

At a loss for words, I nod. He sneers.

"Your professionalism is severely lacking. I'm fairly certain you took more pictures of me than you did the happy couple. Do try and focus on them during the reception. After all, it is your job, Miss Murphy."

His cruel words penetrate my skin and fall over the swarming butterflies like a net, trapping them beneath its suffocating weight. And yet still, all I manage to say is, "You know my name?"

"It's my business to know." He scoffs as he turns and stalks out the door, as though he didn't cut me down at the knees. My only saving grace is everyone is so wrapped up in Stacia and West, they missed our little display.

Shaking off his sour attitude, I lift my camera just in time to see West swat Stacia on her ass as they exit the event space, making all who witness it laugh.

I pull my camera away from my face, quickly checking whether or not I captured the image. I did, but my victory feels a little sour.

Then again, meeting the love of your life and having him hate you on sight tends to put a damper on things.

Story of my freaking life.

CHAPTER 2
COLTON

I try to put the unprofessional, purple-haired hack job out of my mind for the rest of the night. Truly I do, but her presence is inescapable.

Even dressed to blend in, she stands out. The deep navy number she's wearing looks like a dress at first glance but is actually shorts. The lightweight material clings to her, perfectly complementing her long, lean physique. It's absurd, really. Everywhere I look—there she is.

My eyes seem to be drawn to her of their own accord. Again, absurd, as she's not remotely my type. I prefer my women short, curvy, and with something more than hot air occupying the space between their ears. Though, I will say, she seems to have taken my advice to heart and is focusing on the bride and groom, so there's that.

I'm at the bar decidedly *not* watching Miss Murphy when West approaches me, his new wife in tow. "You having a good time?" he asks, slapping me on the back.

"The best," I deadpan, raising my glass to him.

"Smartass," Stacia mutters under her breath. To say it

took the two of us a while to get along is putting it mildly. But in the end, I'm man enough to admit I was wrong—West and Stacia are great together.

"Seriously, though, I'm happy for the two of you. And tonight has been…enjoyable."

West rolls his eyes. "You sure know how to dole out those compliments, don't ya?"

I shrug and finish the last of my whiskey. "Top shelf liquor, a Michelin-star worthy meal, and cake…what could I possibly have to complain about?"

A flash of purple moves in my periphery, as if to remind me not everything's been up to snuff. Glancing over my shoulder, I confirm Miss Murphy is snapping away as we talk. It's on the tip of my tongue to tell West his photographer isn't worth the pretty penny I know she's charging them, but I refrain. It's neither the time nor the place to air such grievances. Plus, I'm not one to bring an accusation to the table without facts to prove it. There's a reason my win record is one of the best in the courtroom, after all.

"You're something else, man," West says, his tone full of mirth. "For real though, I'm glad you're here."

I signal the bartender for another drink. "You're like a brother to me; there's nowhere else I'd rather be."

"You always say I'm a pain in your ass," he counters.

"Pretty sure we're using different words to say the same thing." We chat for a few more minutes until the newlyweds are called away by other guests.

Several long hours later, I'm standing at the curb, waiting on my Uber, tipsy, tired, and beyond ready to head home. A small headache throbs behind my eyes as I check the app on my phone to see how far out my car is.

"Excuse me," a soft voice says from my right.

I turn my head toward the sound. "Miss Murphy," I mutter her name like a curse.

"You can call me Ashley." She takes a step closer. At six-four, I'm used to having to look down when speaking to women, but she can nearly look me in the eyes.

My body pivots toward hers of its own accord. "I'd rather not."

She sucks on her lower lip before licking them both. "I think we may have gotten off on the wrong foot. Could we…perhaps…start over?"

I mull over her offer, but ultimately decline, as my first impressions are rarely ever wrong. "Again, I'd rather not."

A long sigh passes her glossy lips. "Listen, Mister…" she trails off, waiting for me to supply my name.

"Banks. Colton Banks."

The lavender-haired menace breaks into a grin as she offers me her hand to shake. "Ashley Murphy, nice to meet you."

Not wanting to be outright rude or to lie, I remain silent and keep my hands firmly at my sides. After a few breaths, Little Miss Sunshine gets the memo and drops her hand.

"I'm not sure why you're so put off by me…" She swallows roughly. Something tells me she isn't used to people disliking her. I grin, knowing it's probably eating her up inside.

She steps closer, brings her hand to my chest, and

curls her long, delicate fingers around my lapel. "Ugh. I…this…is going to sound out there, but I'd really like to take you out to dinner," she says as she rubs the material of my jacket between her thumb and forefinger, seemingly entranced by the luxurious texture.

I step back from her, dislodging her hold on me. "Absolutely not."

"But—"

I slice my hand through the air, silencing her. "But nothing. Clearly my original assessment of you still stands. You're unprofessional and frankly, quite forward."

She opens her mouth to speak, right as my ride appears. I stalk to the car, fling open the door, and slide into the back seat before she can give life to whatever asinine bullshit apology she was surely about to deliver.

My driver wastes no time pulling back into traffic, and while a small part of me wants to know if Miss Murphy watches us drive away, I refuse to spare her a second glance. As far as I'm concerned, the woman is nothing but trouble. Goodbye and good riddance.

CHAPTER 3
ASHLEY

swear to God, if you don't hand over my wedding pictures, I will run your business into the ground! You will never shoot another wedding in Cottonwood again!"

Tears sting my eyes, and I have to bite down on my tongue to keep from telling Megan Grace Garcia—*yes, she goes by both*—exactly how I feel. Instead, I take a deep breath and try for professionalism instead. "Mrs. Garcia, I'm truly sorry it's come to this. However, until the remainder of your balance is paid, I will be unable to release the photographs to you. It is stated plainly in the contract we both signed."

Phew! Go me!

"And I told you I'm not paying, after the atrocious job you did on my bridal session!"

My right eye twitches. "If you recall, I tried rescheduling due to the inclement weather."

I feel like a broken record at this point. Megan Grace has been calling me twice a day for going on three days now. I had a bad feeling when she and I first met, but ignored it. Talk about having regrets. This bridezilla is every wedding photographer's nightmare come to life.

"I don't see what the weather has to do with an indoor photoshoot! You're a hack, and I'm going to make sure everyone knows it! You're finished! Through!"

She hangs up before I can reply, which is probably a good thing because I'm all out of nice things to say to her. I'm half tempted to throw my phone at the wall, but with how my day is progressing, I'll probably crack the damn screen. I settle for yelling at the top of my lungs instead. There's something cathartic about a good yell.

But even better is having a bitch-fest with your bestie—even if she lives a state away. Thankfully, Mally answers on the first ring. "I only have ten minutes before the kids will be back in my classroom. They are having library time, so talk fast!"

"Ugh! You remember that bad-juju bride I told you about?"

"I do."

"She is a thousand times worse than I ever imagined. She is literally threatening to launch a smear campaign against me and is stalker-calling me multiple times a day!"

Mally sucks in a breath. "No way! What a psycho! What are you gonna do?"

"I honestly don't know what to do. I feel…stuck."

"You want me to ask Duke what he thinks?"

A warm feeling settles in my gut—*gratefulness.* "Oh my glob, yes! That would be amazeballs!"

"Deal," she laughs, "as long as you never say amaze-balls again."

"Hey! That is a classic."

"Classically bad." She laughs harder, and I vow to say the word forever if this is the response it gets. The closed-off, broken shell of a girl I first met is nothing at all like the vibrant woman I have the pleasure of calling my best friend. Mallory's been through hell and back—at least twice—and is one of the strongest human beings I've ever met.

"Pssh. You love it."

"You're a grown ass woman who talks like some weird crossbreed between a middle-aged dad, a hippie, and a VSCO girl."

"Mood." I pitch my voice an octave higher and draw out the word, knowing it will set her off all over again.

"Oh my God! Stop it. What does that even mean?"

"It is a way to express relatability."

"Ash, what have I told you about reading the Urban Dictionary for fun?"

"Whatever. You freaking love me!"

"I totally do. Crap! I gotta go!"

"Thanks for letting me vent."

"Anytime. I'll let you know what Duke says. Love you big."

"Love you bigger." I tap the end call button and toss my phone down onto my desk, feeling a little lighter than I did before.

Said light feeling disintegrates a few hours later after posting a stunning photo from the Larson wedding to my Instagram as a sneak peek.

It is absolutely one of the best images I've ever taken, and the redhead's natural beauty only makes it that much better. I wouldn't be shocked if it went viral, with how attractive Stacia and West are.

Within seconds of me posting it, comments begin rolling in. Only, instead of the virtual high-fives I'm used to getting, the thread is riddled with cruelty.

Tears gather along my lashes as I read line after line of vitriol. Shock, hurt, anger, and confusion all push for dominance within me. Confusion pulls ahead in the race until I see a comment from Bridezilla herself, Megan Grace.

Suddenly, it all makes sense. She said she was going to ruin me, and it seems like she's recruited every single Petty Betty she's ever crossed paths with to help further her little online hate-fest.

It would be one thing for these wenches to attack my business—and they are—but they're going beyond and talking shit about my clients, which is something I will not tolerate. These awful women are taking every cheap shot they can find, picking her apart in the worst way possible. One nutjob called Stacia a slut because her dress showed off her curves, while another said she must be the paid help because there's no way a man like West would go for her. They trash her tattoos and her dress, and joke about her hair color.

I'm torn between wanting to sob and vomit. Being a woman is hard enough without all the Megan Graces of the world calling in favors from their Mean Girl Brigade.

Jesus-I-need-some-chips-and-queso-dip-Christ.

I allow myself exactly seven minutes of wallowing before putting on my big girl panties and getting to work on damage control.

Step one: ordering takeout from Los Tacos. *Whoever*

invented food delivery, blessings to you and all of your future offspring.

Step two: sending screenshots to Mallory.

Step three: contacting the Larsons, as painful as it may be. I run my business on integrity, and I won't allow them to stumble upon that thread blindly.

Step four: find a lawyer.

I breeze through the first two items on my list and hopefully by the time I finish this next phone call, I'll have a heaping order of nachos—with extra queso—all to myself.

My hands are unsteady as I scroll to Stacia's contact card in my phone. She answers on the third ring. "Hey, Ashley!" Her voice is bright and clear.

"Hey." I decide to skip the small talk and pleasantries. "As you know, my reputation is everything to me."

Her throaty laughter trickles through the line. "Uh, yeah. That's one of the reasons I hired you."

"Right. Well." I take a deep breath. "I'm very particular about who I work with, and, long story short, I booked a bride when I shouldn't have, and it is fast becoming a nightmare. She has a vendetta against me and is determined to run my business into the ground."

"I'm so sorry," Stacia says, genuine concern coating her words. "That's horrible."

"It gets worse. She's going beyond attacking my business now. She is going after my clients as well—namely you and West, since my most recent posts have been from y'all's wedding."

"Oh, hell no!" Stacia roars with a ferocity that almost makes me drop my phone.

She's pissed. My career is probably over. FML. "I assure

you, any and all disparaging remarks about you and your family will be removed. I know—"

"Fuck that twat."

"What?" I ask, because I couldn't have heard her right.

"Fuck her. I'm reading the comments now. A bunch of country-club-going, fake-tan-having, can't-smile-from-too-much-Botox bitches are the least of my worries."

"What?" Ninety-nine percent sure I sound like a broken record, but if she's not upset about what people are saying about her, then what?

"There's no way we're about to let some bored-ass housewife who's going to be divorced before her first anniversary ruin you. Hell no."

"I'm not sure I'm following."

Stacia laughs softly. "Ashley, I'm not worried about what these keyboard warriors have to say about me or my family. We know who we are; their words can't hurt us, and they certainly don't define us. But they *can* hurt you and your business. I'm not okay with that. I won't stand for it. Which is why I'm going to help you."

"Oh, I-I wasn't calling to ask for help, just to make you aware of the situation. I didn't want you or your husband to stumble across it."

Stacia shushes me. "Nope. Women—*real women*—stand beside one another. They support one another. And, Ashley, I'm about to support the fuck out of you. First thing you need to do is contact Colton Banks."

My stomach drops. "Do you happen to know any other lawyers?"

"What? Why? He's by far the best lawyer in the county. Hell, maybe even the state."

I clear my throat as dread settles in my gut. "I, um, I just don't think hiring him is the best idea."

"Don't be silly. He's West's best friend and will make sure this bologna gets buried."

"Pretty sure he'd rather bury me," I mumble under my breath.

Of course, Stacia hears me. "Why would you say that?"

"We…may…have had a run-in at your wedding."

"Don't let his prickliness fool you. He's a softy inside. Trust me. I'll get West to talk to him, but go see him. Please?"

Maybe she's right, maybe his frosty exterior is a defense mechanism. "Okay, I'll do it."

"Promise?"

"Promise," I say, knowing full well I'm going to end up regretting it.

CHAPTER 4
ASHLEY

To say I wasn't expecting Colton to work in the center of Cottonwood's cozy downtown would be putting it mildly. Furthering my shock, his office is smackdab next door to the yoga studio I take weekly classes at.

Small world, smaller town.

I linger outside the pale purple door—the color is eerily similar to my hair—trying like hell to convince myself this isn't an epic mistake in the making.

Gathering my courage, I pull open the door and walk inside. I don't even make it two steps before a deep, masculine voice stops me in my tracks.

"No! Absolutely not."

My stomach churns. "But you don't even know why I'm here!"

His blue eyes pin me from across the room. "And I don't care either. Leave." Colton's tone never waivers, which honestly makes him all the scarier.

"Colt—Mr. Banks—please. Five minutes. No, four!

Just give me four minutes, surely you can spare me that."

He clenches his jaw, stands from his desk, and stalks my way. "Make it two."

I nod, my head bobbing lamely like a dashboard figurine.

"Your time starts now, Miss Murphy."

"Right! A bride is threatening to sue me! I didn't want to work with her to start with. She gave me bad vibes, and them together...let's just say they're not built to last. But she was persistent, and eventually, I relented, and she signed the contract and paid the deposit for the deluxe wedding package on the spot. But, on the day of her bridal pics—which we were doing at my studio—it was raining. *Talk about a bad omen*, right?"

I shiver.

"Anyway, I tried rescheduling because I don't use artificial lighting. It is *so* not my style. The clouds were completely covering the sun, so it was super doom and gloom. But she refused and demanded we do them anyway.

"She wasn't happy with the pictures. She said they were too dark—well, no shit, Karen, it was practically pitch-black outside—and here's the kicker, I've already shot her wedding, and now she's refusing to pay the rest of her fee. So, obviously, I'm not giving her any pictures. And now she's threatening to sue me and is dragging me through the mud on social media!"

By the time I'm finished, my chest is heaving and sweat beads along my hairline. Detached indifference swims in Colton's eyes, but he remains mute. So, I continue. "Stacia said you were the best and so, help?" I wring my hands and lick my lips. "Please?"

He wavers, and for a split-second, I think he's going to give in. He sucks in a breath and bows his head. "Ah, sorry. No can do." He strides across the room like he owns it—and I guess he does—moving right past me to the semi-open door. "I'd like to say it was nice seeing you, but, frankly, it wasn't. Let's not do this again anytime soon. Best of luck to you, Miss Murphy."

I flinch back, trying to dislodge the stupid stinging behind my eyes. I will not cry in front of this self-important jackass. Straightening my spine, I mentally fix my crown and step back out onto the sidewalk.

"I'm not giving up!" I shout as he slams the pretty purple door behind me. Asshole or not, Stacia said he was the best, and something tells me, I'm going to need to be on my A-game to take on Megan Grace.

If I'm being totally honest, I'm determined to work with him now, if only to spite him. He thinks he's above me. That he's better than me. That I'm *unprofessional* and *forward* and probably a million other things. Too bad for him I'm also clever, crafty, and really fucking persistent.

Shaking with anger over his easy dismissal and harsh judgments, I stalk over to Main Street Yoga and sign up for an emergency class.

Ninety minutes later, I emerge dripping in sweat and more determined than ever. Breaking Colton down will be a difficult task, but so was mastering my Tittibhasana —or Firefly Pose. I've never been one to shy away from a little bit of hard work, and I'm not about to start now. Especially with my livelihood on the line.

Colton Banks doesn't have a clue of what's about to hit him. By the time I'm done, he'll not only agree to represent me, he'll see we're soulmates, too.

With my laptop balanced on my knees, I recline back in my cozy, burnt orange corduroy chair and wait for Mallory's Skype call. I texted her after my emergency yoga class to give her an update, and we agreed to Skype after dinner.

At six on the dot, she calls. "Hello, fair maiden!" I greet her with a goofy grin.

"I hope you don't mind; the girls are here, too!"

"Not at all," I say, waving to Jenny and Natalie. The four of us catch up and coo over Mallory and Natalie's pregnant bellies before diving into the crux of our call.

"So, Mally says you're having some boy trouble?" Jenny asks.

I smile as I recall the first time I ever spoke to the bombshell blonde. Mallory was interested in renting her cottage and was going out to look at it, and since I couldn't be there in person, I demanded she bring me along via video chat, and the rest was history. I even drove to Alabama to shoot Jenny's wedding to Natalie's older brother Nate.

"Yeah, spill!" Natalie says, using her mom voice.

I quickly catch them up on everything that's transpired, from Megan Grace, to Colton telling me off at the wedding, and him rejecting me again this afternoon. By the time I finish, I'm wound up and spitting mad all over again.

"Wait," Jenny says, leaning toward the screen. "He actually called you *forward*? How old is he? Sixty?"

"Ugh. No. He's…well, I'm not sure. I would say close to my age. He'd be drop-dead gorgeous if weren't for the giant stick up his ass."

"Gorgeous, huh? You never mentioned he was attractive."

I glare at my best friend. "His excessive good looks are a moot point. The issue is I need to find a way to convince him to represent me."

"The answer is obvious," Natalie says. "You need insider info."

"Ooh, yes!" Mallory agrees. "Do you think your client who is friends with him would help?"

I turn the idea over in my head a few times. "It couldn't hurt to ask."

The girls and I chat for a few more minutes before Natalie's daughter needs help with her homework.

After we end the chat, I pick up my phone and text Stacia.

ME

Hey, Stacia. Things didn't go over so well with Colton today, and I was hoping you could maybe help me out.

She calls instead of texting me back. "Hey," I say hesitantly, hoping I didn't somehow overstep.

"What do you mean it didn't go well?"

"He flat-out told me he wouldn't help me and that he never wanted to see me again."

She clucks her tongue. "God, he's an insufferable jackass. I literally hated him when we first met."

"Yeah…he's a real peach." I move my laptop over to

the table and tuck my legs underneath me. "Any advice on buttering him up?"

"Can you cook?"

"Yeah." I nod as I say the words.

"Food, then. He works stupid hours and typically eats out. Make him something homemade and delicious."

"What kind of food does he like?"

"He really likes sweets."

"Like candy?"

"Candy, cakes, chocolate, you name it."

"Huh. Never would have guessed someone so salty would have a sweet tooth."

Stacia laughs. "Salty and sweet, am I right?"

"Too true."

CHAPTER 5
COLTON

Four days have passed since the purple-haired menace barged into my office and demanded I help her. Much to my displeasure, she's still on my mind. It's as if she's hijacked my thoughts and is holding them for ransom.

Which is the only semi-logical reason the sight of her standing outside my office, bright and early on a Monday morning, has my lips tipping up in a slight grin.

She's yet to notice me, a fact I take advantage of as I slow my approach and study her. She's dressed in black overalls with a daisy print and a yellow sleeveless top underneath. Her ridiculously colored hair is piled on top of her head in a messy wad and comically large sunglasses obscure most of her face.

I clear my throat as I approach, and she looks my way.

"Oh, good! You're here."

"What are you doing here, Miss Murphy?"

She keeps on, as if I didn't just ask her a direct question. "I wasn't sure what time you started your day, so I made sure to get here early."

Changing tactics, I ask, "How long have you been here?"

"Since six." She shrugs, as if it's completely normal for her to loiter outside of my office for nearly an hour.

"You're exhibiting stalker-like tendencies. Have you considered talking to a professional?"

Much to my surprise, she laughs. "Oh, yes, I see a therapist at least once a month."

"Then maybe up it to bimonthly."

Unbothered, she simply smiles. Idly, I wonder what exactly it would take to knock that happy-go-lucky grin off her pretty, pouty lips. "Would you mind stepping aside? Some of us have actual work to do."

"Sure thing, Colton."

"Mr. Banks," I correct her as I slide the key into the lock and open the door. I stride inside, flipping the lights on as I go. Like a lonely stray puppy, she follows.

I carry on, business as usual, and brew myself an espresso before taking a seat behind my desk. Once I'm situated, I spin my chair to face her. "Is there a reason for your visit?"

She steps forward, holding a small picnic basket of sorts out toward me. "I came by to bring you these."

I eye her and the offering skeptically. "And these are…"

"Take a look." She places the basket down onto my desk.

As gently as possible, I pull back the yellow cloth covering the contents.

"It's not a bomb, you know?" she drawls.

I scowl and pull back the cloth the rest of the way.

My mouth instantly waters on sight, but when the smell of decadent chocolate hits me, I'm a goner. However, on principle alone, I place the basket on my desk and push it toward her. "No, thank you."

"Cheesecake chocolate chip muffins. Freshly made from scratch this morning."

"How industrious of you."

"Delicious is the word you're looking for. Go on." She nudges them back my way. "Try them."

"I'd rather not," I tell her, lying through my teeth.

"It's not like I poisoned them."

I blink slowly. Poison…there's something I hadn't considered. Wouldn't put it past her, though. "Miss Murphy, in the short time I've known you, I've witnessed unprofessional behavior, been hit on, solicited, and now you're here pushing food of unknown origin on me. Surely you can see why I'm not interested."

"Solicited? Excuse me? I'm not a prostitute."

Inexplicably, arousal stirs within me. "In the sense of business. You have solicited my business. Your sex life is not on my radar."

Her cheeks pinken. "Oh. Right. Well, whatever. My muffins are bomb." She leans forward and plucks one out of the basket and brings it to her lips. She inhales deeply before taking a bite. "Mmmm," she moans, licking the chocolate crumbs from her lips. "Delicious."

I'm torn between kicking her out and demanding she finish the rest of the muffin right here in front of me. Ashley Murphy may not be anywhere near my type, but somehow, she makes the simple task of eating seem erotic.

"Your loss," she says, reaching for the basket.

I knock her hand away. "Leave the muffins," I growl.

Ashley purses her lips to hide her grin. "Have a great day, Colton." She skips toward the door. "I mean, Mr. Banks." She winks, stepping outside, leaving me frustrated—in more ways than one.

An hour later the stupid muffin basket still taunts me. After Ashley left, I stood with the intent to chuck them in the trash. Somehow, they ended up on the table next to my coffee machine. Now every time I refill my mug, the yellow cloth covering the baked goods all but laughs at me.

Two hours in, I feel like the man from Poe's "The Tell-Tale Heart," only instead of a dismembered body beneath my floorboards, I have a wicker basket of chocolate cheesecake treats on my fucking console table.

By hour three, I can't take it any longer. The godforsaken muffins have to go. I stalk across the room and snatch up the basket, feeling crazed. I'm a grown man—this shouldn't be affecting me like this, and yet I'm helpless to stop it.

As I move toward the back door, the fan in the corner of the room blows the scent of cinnamon sugar and chocolate my way. It's an alluring mixture of the baker and her creation.

It's also my breaking point.

I grab a muffin and bite into it. It's every bit as good as she boasted. The cream cheese filling is decadent. The chocolate, divine. It's over the top and sweet enough to leave cavities in its wake. They're one of the best things I've ever eaten, and that only pisses me off all the more.

Ashley Murphy and her delicious muffins can go right to hell.

Tuesday morning, I approach my office with caution, as if I'm liable to be sneak-attacked by my—I mean, the—purple-haired menace; she's not *my* anything. However, I seem to be in the clear.

I spend the first part of my day on pins and needles, but by lunchtime, I'm feeling pretty confident that Ashley has given up.

At twelve on the dot, I head out the door to meet a client for lunch. She requested we meet at Basil's—a local Greek place—which happens to be a favorite of mine.

Over hummus and gyros, we go over the terms of the software sale agreement presented to her by the company wanting to purchase the rights to the dating app she designed. I go through it with a fine-toothed comb, marking the areas I think she either needs to push back on or refuse outright. Before I know it, two hours have passed, and it's time for us to part ways. I quickly settle the bill and tell my client I'll be in touch when I hear back from our negotiations.

Back at my office, I dive into paperwork, drafting an email with our proposed revisions. I'm in the middle of my second read-through when the front door flies open.

"May I help you?" I ask the plainclothes courier.

"Are you Colton Banks?"

"I am."

"Be right back." The young man steps out and re-enters with a...*is that a fucking bouquet of...who the fuck would send me flowers?* He sets the massive arrangement on the coffee table in my waiting room. "Sign here," he says, holding a small tablet out toward me.

I scrawl my name in the designated box, effectively dismissing him in favor of the fragrant blooms now perfuming my entire office. There's a card tucked between the stems; I grab it and flip it open.

> *Colton (I mean Mr. Banks),*
> *Your attitude about helping me kind of stinks. Maybe these will help.*
> *-Ashley (A.K.A. Miss Murphy)*

I swear to God, this woman is singlehandedly driving me to the brink of insanity. Rage sizzles through my veins as I dial West's number. He doesn't answer, but I'm annoyed enough to try again and immediately redial.

"Stalk much?" he asks upon answering.

"Miss Murphy's number. Now."

West's laughter grates on my ears. "Now, Colton, is that how we ask for something we want?"

This motherfucker is dad-voicing me. "I'm not your son, West. Give me the number."

"You're sure acting like him. Calling twice in a row to demand a phone number is right up there with Asher banging his cup on the table when he wants more juice."

"Weston!"

"Joke's on both of y'all, though. All you gotta do is ask nicely. More flies with honey and all."

"I hate you."

"Hmm. Still didn't hear those magic words. Call me back when you find your manners." He hangs up on me, and it takes my all not to slam my phone into the wall.

I call back, and when he answers, I say what he wants to hear through clenched teeth. "May I please have Ashley's phone number?"

"I already texted it to you. Sucker."

I hang up on him this time, rethinking our friendship for the millionth time.

CHAPTER 6
ASHLEY

'm hard at work retouching photos when my phone rings. The number is unfamiliar, but most of the people calling me are potential clients, so I answer.

"Hello, this is Ashley."

"Am I supposed to find your antics clever?" A growly yet refined voice barks in my ear. *Colton.*

"Actually, you're supposed to say 'thank you.' Or are you one of those men who feels emasculated by receiving flowers?"

"No, I'm the kind of man who isn't swayed by paltry attempts at bribery."

Why would fate assign me such a monumental jackass as my soulmate? Clearly the universe has a sick sense of humor. "Good thing I'm not trying to bribe you, then," I say, lying through my teeth.

"Aren't you, though? Muffins, flowers, what's next? Maybe a box of chocolates? Half of your peanut butter sandwich? I'm not your grade school crush. I'm a professional, Miss Murphy, and only work with other professionals, which you have demonstrated time and time again, you are not."

I tap the speaker button on my phone and toss it down on my desk. This man makes me insane. "You are truly the most condescending man I've ever met. You don't know me well enough to have formed these kinds of opinions about me."

In all honesty, his extreme dislike of me hurts. A lot. Especially with how my heart and soul long for his. He means for his words to dissuade me—to break me—but every single insult and rebuff only makes me want to prove him wrong that much more.

"They say the truth hurts, Miss Murphy. It's not my fault you're ill-equipped to handle the pain."

I clench my fists so tightly my nails dig into my palms, leaving behind little crescent-shaped marks. This man makes me want to commit felonies—you know, like murder. *I wonder, since he's my soulmate, could it be classed as a crime of passion?* "I can handle everything you dish out and more."

Colton makes a noise low in his throat, and I can nearly picture the sneer on his face. "Is that a threat?"

"It's a promise, Mr. Banks. Do your worst; I'll not only take it—I'll return it back tenfold."

"You don't have it in you." He laughs cruelly, the dark tenor of it winding around my heart in inky swirls.

"I'm far stronger than you give credit for." Not to mention, my plan of attack is to repay his barbs with kindness. Something tells me that will knock him off guard far more than volleying back with harsh words or petty.

"You mistake strength for stupidity."

"And you underestimate me." I end the call before he

can reply, crumpling down to my desk chair with my heart thundering and my pulse racing.

I'll show that sexy, arrogant jackass exactly who he's up against. I may be quirky and kind, but those two qualities are exactly what give me an edge. Colton Banks is used to sharks and snakes, but he's about to be brought to his knees by a creature far more deadly—a woman scorned.

Two days later, I'm meeting Stacia for lunch at a little diner called Benny's to deliver the portrait I had wood-printed from my favorite snap from her wedding day. It's a breathtaking candid of her, West, and Asher.

I always present my clients with a gift when delivering the flash drive containing their images. I offer them an online viewing gallery as well, but to me, it's little touches like this that set me apart from the competition.

In addition to surprising her with this post-wedding gift, I'm also hoping to get a little more insider info on Colton Holier-Than-Thou Banks.

The diner is cute, with a throwback retro look. There's a line at the door and every single seat is occupied, save for the one across from the redhead I'm here to meet.

"Hi, I'm meeting her," I say to the hostess, nodding my head toward Stacia. She passes me a menu as I move through the line to the table.

"Hey, girl!" Stacia says over the rim of her coffee mug.

"Hi!" I offer the slim, neatly wrapped box to her before sliding into my chair. "This is for you."

Her deep brown eyes twinkle with a mixture of joy and curiosity. "What's this?"

"Open it," I urge her.

I watch, raptly, as she peels back the paper. This is one of the best parts of my job—surprising my clients with little things like this.

"Oh," she breathes out the word. "My God. This is stunning. Thank you. Truly."

"You are so very welcome. I could photograph your family every day and never grow bored. Really, we should probably schedule vow renewal photoshoots every five years." I wink and she grins.

"Girl, you can take my picture any day. You're a fucking wizard with that camera. Gah! I wish I'd have hired you to take my pictures when I submitted them to Virtual Kitty."

My brows crinkle. "What's that?"

Her grin turns wicked. "West's porn app."

It takes a lot to shock me speechless, but that's exactly what Stacia's done. "His what now?" I finally manage. "Seriously, I need more information."

After we order—french toast and bacon for both of us—Stacia goes on to tell me all about submitting her X-rated pictures to her now-husband's company.

"And you had no idea it was his company?"

"Truly! I just needed the money and knew they paid well."

"This is amazing. Talk about a story to tell your grandkids. Uh...you know, when they're grown." We both dissolve into a fit of giggles.

Once our laughter subsides, Stacia turns solemn. "How are things with Colton?"

"Ugh." I groan at the mention of his name. Honestly, I'm glad she brought him up, but still, he drives me half mad. "He is so pompous. So egotistical. So rude! He makes my—"

"Panties wet?" Stacia supplies, cutting me off.

"I was going to say head hurt."

She shimmies her shoulders. "Something tells me it's both."

I bury my face in my hands.

"Hey, it's okay," she says, her voice softer than before. "There's nothing wrong with being attracted to him."

"It's more than that," I mumble, regretting the words as soon as they slip from my lips.

"What do you mean?"

"No, nothing. Forget it."

"Ah, ah!" She wags her finger at me. "Not happening. You can't say something like that and expect me to walk away."

"No, really. It is so unprofessional for me to even talk to you like this." Heat blossoms in my chest and tears sting my eyes. Colton's right—*I am unprofessional.*

With my mini breakdown impossible to hide, Stacia pays the check and ushers me out the door. Linking her arm with mine, she sets off to glob-knows-where. And for some unknown reason, I let her guide me.

Five minutes later, we're approaching what appears to be an old, converted factory building. "Where are we?" I ask.

"My friend AJ's house."

"She was your matron of honor, right?"

"Yup."

I nod, following behind her *physically* but not quite following her *mentally*. "Okay, but why?"

"Honestly," she says, worrying her lip between her teeth, "you look like you could use a friend or two."

It's on the tip of my tongue to tell her she's wrong, but, deep down, she isn't. Mallory is irreplaceable as my bestie, but I know expanding my tribe a little certainly couldn't hurt. Especially with everything going on right now with Colton and Megan Grace.

"Thank you."

"No worries." She offers me a full-on smile as she punches the call button for the elevator. "Plus, AJ's practically a married old maid; she'll surely have some insight for you."

Any trepidation I had about meeting AJ outside of a professional setting melted away when she answered the front door dressed in her husband's boxer shorts, a crop top, and fuzzy slippers—at noon on a Thursday. Clearly the woman was my kind of people.

"Would you ladies like anything to drink?"

"Stop acting like Miss Manners and put on some coffee," Stacia says, waltzing past her friend into the cozy, industrial-chic apartment.

"Whatever," AJ sasses back, heading into the kitchen with the two of us hot on her heels.

Over several cups of coffee, Stacia and AJ drag everything out of me. From the psycho-bride and her vendetta against me to the asshole attorney who is meant to be my everything but wants jack-all to do with me.

I spill it all.

"Sounds like a witch hunt," AJ says once I'm done.

"It so is," Stacia agrees. "Homegirl is crazy. Ever since she attacked me on the picture you posted, I've been checking daily. She and her mean girl posse are dedicated to their cause."

I shake my head. "Too bad they won't use their powers for good instead of evil."

"Enough about malicious Megan." Stacia fixes me with indecipherable look. "Let's talk about Colton."

"What about him? The fact that he hates me?" I sigh. "Or maybe his refusal to work with me?"

"Or that you wanna take his uptight ass to bone town." AJ looks pensive while Stacia cracks up at her own joke.

"Have you considered fucking him?"

Now I'm laughing. "Did you miss the part about him hating me? And I mean that literally."

She waves her hand in the air as if swatting away a fly. "Hate sex can be a real game changer."

Stacia snorts. "You'd know."

"Damn straight," she says to her best friend before focusing on me. "For real, though, if a good, sweaty, angry sheet sesh isn't on the table, keep up the bribing."

"You think? I actually had an idea, but it might be stupid."

"Let's hear it," Stacia encourages.

"I snapped a picture of him and West at the wedding before you walked down the aisle. It's…hang on." I grab my phone from my bag and pull up the image before showing them my screen. "Here, look."

The image shows the two men in a candid moment,

with their arms around each other and their heads tipped back in laughter.

"Oh, wow," Stacia breathes while AJ nods her agreement. "This is amazing."

"What's the idea?" AJ asks.

I lay it out for the vibrant women before me, and together, the three of us come up with what I'm hoping is a foolproof plan.

CHAPTER 7
COLTON

brought tacos!" West says as he steps into my office.

"Did we have plans today?" I ask, looking from my friend down to my calendar.

"Taco Tuesday." He says it as if it is reason alone to barge into my office in the middle of a work day.

Still, a free meal… "You remember extra lime wedges?"

"Yes, your majesty." He drops the paper bag down onto my desk and sniffs the air. "It smells different in here."

Inwardly, I groan. Over the course of the last twelve days, Miss Murphy has sent two more bouquets, along with more baked goods than I could possibly ever consume—each one more enjoyable than the last. She also had coffee delivered on two different occasions.

The woman has an uncanny ability to anticipate my needs—that or she truly is stalking me. I admit I'm impressed with her persistence.

Opting to ignore West's comment, I snatch up the

bag and retrieve my food, my mouth watering already. I lift the delicious concoction to my mouth, ready to dig in, when he starts up again.

"Really, are you using a new air freshener?" he asks.

I sigh and let my food drop back to the wax paper wrapper on my desk, red cabbage spilling out. "No, I'm not using a new air freshener, or a candle, a plug-in, or potpourri."

"What is it then? Stacia would love it."

"Flowers," I deadpan. "It's fucking flowers."

"Flowers, huh?" West's eyes crinkle as he smiles. "Never took you as a flower kind of guy."

"I'm not." I rewrap my taco and take a bite. The pure rapture of the flavors busting across my tongue is almost enough to drown out my best friend's pointless commentary. Unfortunately, he, too, is persistent.

"Really? Then why are there"—he pretends to look around the space and count— "three *floral* arrangements?" His keen gaze never wavers as he regards me.

Of course, he's in on it. Why the fuck wouldn't he be?

"I take it you're a part of this?"

He whistles innocently. "Of what?"

I pin him with a glare. "Don't play games with me."

Like the happy-go-lucky dumbass he is, West bats his lashes. "Who, me? Never."

I swallow the last bite of my taco and pinch the bridge of my nose, counting down from ten. When I hit one and still want to throttle him, I start over, this time at twenty.

Before I make it back to one, the door flies open as yet another unwanted visitor saunters in.

"Oh, I didn't realize you'd be in a meeting," Ashley says, shifting her grip on the kraft-paper-wrapped package she's clutching to her chest. "I can come back later."

"No worries, it's not a meeting, just lunch between friends," West says, ever the shit-stirrer.

"Are you sure?"

I throw my hands up in the air. "Why bother pretending to care?"

A hurt look crosses Ashley's features. "I do care."

I push away from my desk and stalk toward her. "Oh, you care? Really?"

She nods.

Wisely, West stays seated and silent, his blue eyes pinging between us like he's courtside for a tennis match between Serena Williams and Karolina Pliskova.

"You have a strange way of showing it." I press forward, stepping closer and closer until her back hits the wall and I've boxed her in.

Momentarily, that honeyed fragrance of hers distracts me. She smells good enough to eat. Before I can do something truly insane, like burying my face into her neck and licking her to see if she tastes as sweet as she smells, I come to my senses.

I pull my head back a fraction and glare at her. "You show up randomly with no appointment. You're ceaseless in your attempts at bribery. Honestly, I find this whole thing tiring."

Her lip quivers, but her eyes blaze, though she doesn't try to defend herself.

"You're bordering on pathetic." The words feel wrong, even as I say them, though I'm not sure why. "Please, Miss Murphy, find a new hobby, because your time pestering me has come to an end. If you show up here uninvited again, there will be consequences."

I expect her to cower and apologize. However, the slender spitfire wastes no time proving me wrong. She places her palms flat to my chest and shoves me back. "You know what? You're right. I was trying to butter you up, bribe you, whatever. Stacia was adamant that you were the best. But as far as I can see, the only thing you're good at is belittling those around you."

Her words create an unfamiliar hollow feeling in my gut, but she doesn't relent.

"You're so quick to call me unprofessional and deluded and glob knows what else. But I'm done. Done! I've already got one hateful person trying to destroy my business and reputation—I don't need another, fate be damned. Have a nice life, asshole."

She shoves all the way past me, tossing a farewell to West just before breezing back out onto the sidewalk.

As the door closes, I notice she left behind the package she had been carrying. Not wanting her to have a reason to return, I grab it and run after her. "Miss Murphy!" I shout her name, and she spins to face me.

"What?"

"You forgot—"

"I didn't forget anything, Mr. Banks. Consider it a token of my unprofessionalism."

She turns her back to me and rushes across the street. I watch her, with something akin to guilt swirling within me, until she is safely behind the wheel of her garish orange Subaru.

Back inside, I waste no time tearing in the package she left behind. What I find beneath the pristine wrapping steals my breath away. Ashley Murphy is decidedly not a hack. She's the real deal, with more talent in her index finger than most have in their entire being. She's not just taking photos; she's capturing memories and immortalizing them.

Looking at this print of West and myself, I'm hit with every single emotion I was feeling when it was taken.

Happiness and pride for my best friend, uncertainty for the future, and secret longing to have something similar. *I'll take the last two with me to the grave before speaking them out loud.*

"It's amazing, right?" West asks, looking at the canvas over my shoulder. "She has this ability to…stop time with her shutter."

I nod, because he's exactly right. She finds the exceptional in the ordinary and brings it to life with her camera. "She's as talented as she is gorgeous—" *When in the hell did I decide she was gorgeous?*

"You wanna run that by me one more time?"

I shake my head. "Not particularly."

West hums under his breath. "It sounds like you find Ashley attractive. Gorgeous…that's what you said, right?"

"Enough," I growl, not bothering to reply. We both know what I said, repeating myself will only give him more of a reason to gloat—the asshole's ego is already at max capacity.

CHAPTER 8
ASHLEY

The sound of my phone ringing pulls me from the land of dreams and back into the real world.

The sun is high in the sky and shining through the slats of my blinds, causing me to blink rapidly as I check my phone to see who could possibly be calling me at the ungodly hour of—I squint and bring the phone closer—eleven o'clock in the morning.

Colton Banks, that's who.

The question is why. Why is he calling me?

"Hello," I yawn into the phone as I stretch across my mattress.

"Were you sleeping?" Disbelief weighs heavy in his tone.

"Mmm, yep."

"You do realize it's nearly time for lunch, right?"

"And you do realize," I say, mimicking his snooty tone, "that my sleeping habits are none of your business?"

He sighs. "I didn't call to fight."

I shift and sit up against my upholstered headboard. "Then why did you call?"

"Several reasons."

My eyes roll back far enough to see my own skull. "And would you like to share those reasons?"

"Right. First, I'd like to thank you for the canvas print of West and me. It's phenomenal, and I'm man enough to admit I was wrong. Second, I would like to offer my services. It's my opinion we should start with a cease and desist letter—"

"I'm going to go ahead and stop you. While I appreciate hearing you eat crow, I'm no longer in need of your representation in any way. Thank you for calling, though."

"What do you mean?" His voice has a hardness that sets my teeth on edge. *This is a post-coffee call if there ever was one.*

"I meant what I said. I am meeting with another lawyer tomorrow."

"Who?"

"Why does it matter?" I ask as I shuffle into the kitchen in search of caffeine.

"Do not test me."

I huff out an exasperated sigh as I punch the *brew* button. "I'm not testing you. It's just not really your business."

"Ashley." He softens his voice. "Please tell me."

"If it means ending this conversation sooner rather than later, sure. I'm meeting with Danny Williams."

"The fuck you are," he growls, sounding nearly feral.

"Excuse me?"

"You are not going to meet with him." He speaks as though he's the final authority. *Yeah-fucking-right.*

"Last I checked, you aren't my daddy. What are you gonna do? Take me over you knee and spank me?"

"There's a thought," he mutters.

My cheeks burn at the implication. Surely, he doesn't mean—of course he doesn't; he's told me time and time again I'm not his type. Which royally sucks, seeing as he's exactly mine. Soulmate, that is. *Talk about a colossal fuck-up, Universe!*

"Ashley, please. Danny is a snake. Meeting with him is a mistake."

I shrug even though he can't see me. "Mistakes are part of life. Maybe this will be one and maybe it won't. Thanks for…looking out for me, though?" I phrase it like a question, because why in the hell would this man look out for me?

He groans, his aggravation coming through loud and clear. "He has a reputation—"

"Colton," I cut him off. "You have made it abundantly clear, time and time again, that you have no desire to work with me. I pushed when I shouldn't have, for my own selfish reasons. I think our best bet going forward is as…polite acquaintances."

He scoffs.

"I'd say friends, but I don't think you'd go for it."

"You wanna be friends?" He asks it in such a way it feels more like a threat. "Then let's be friends."

"Uh. Sure."

"Great. So, as a friend, I'm asking you not to meet Danny."

Now I'm scoffing. "That's not how friendships work, Colton. Now, I have a hot bath and an even hotter cup of coffee calling my name. Talk later." I end the call before he can reply.

The following day, I'm heading out the door for my consultation with Mr. Williams. We're meeting at a local Brazilian steakhouse, so even if our meeting is a bust, the food will be good.

I arrive ten minutes before the scheduled time to find him here and waiting—a good sign, I hope.

After brief introductions, where his handshake lingers a little too long for my preference, the hostess leads us to a table in the center of the restaurant. She lets us know our server will be along shortly and leaves us to look over the menus.

"Tell me about your little issue," he asks, his eyes on my breasts rather than the menu.

"It's actually a rather large issue. The bride is amping up her attacks against me daily. She has escalated from commenting on my posts to reporting my page and my ads. She has people emailing me hate mail and others calling, spewing unthinkably cruel words when I answer. I'm to the point now where I won't pick up unless I know the number."

"Uh huh." His eyes flit to mine before dropping to my lips and then back down to my breasts. To say I feel uncomfortable is an understatement.

Maybe Colton was right about this guy…

"So, she's being mean to you on the internet because you botched her pictures?"

Red colors my vision at this man's nerve. Luckily, our waitress appears, saving me from tearing him a new one in front of all of the other patrons.

"Hello, I'm Shain, and I'll be taking care of y'all today. Our specials are—"

Mr. Williams cuts her off with a wave of his beefy hand. "We'll each take a vodka soda. I'll have the filet, and she'll have the green salad."

I bristle. "Actually—"

He waves his paw of a hand through the air again, this time shooing our waitress away.

"I wanted a steak as well," I tell him.

"Gotta watch that figure," he replies, and I clench my fists. *This man is an imbecile.* "Now, the thing is, doll-face, this lady has the right to free speech. You can't stop her from saying how she feels. Even if it hurts your feelings."

I place my palms flat down on the table, glaring at him as I speak, barely keeping my anger in check. "It is far more than my *feelings* being hurt, Mr. Williams. This is slander—no, this is *libel*. She is after me with a pitchfork when all I've done is upheld a contract we both signed."

Licking his lips, he looks me up and down, his eyes trailing over me in a way that leaves me feeling dirty. "I'll tell you what, I think I can make this whole thing go away."

His sudden change in attitude gives me pause. "Okay…" I say hesitantly. "How?"

"I'll need my retainer plus a little something extra. A favor of sorts."

Red flags wave and alarm bells blare in my mind. "A favor?"

He shoots me a predatory grin. "An oral favor."

It takes my all not to gag. This man truly is deplorable. "Are you asking me to suck your dick in return for professional services?" I shove my chair back and stand, not giving time to answer. "You're disgusting!"

"Now, hold on!" He pushes back and stands as well, reaching for me.

I turn to flee, only to run smack dab into a solid wall of…muscle. "You're okay," a deep, familiar voice says.

"Colton?" I say, tilting my head a fraction of an inch to look at him.

"Let's go," he murmurs down to me, his voice softer than I've ever heard.

And just this once, instead of arguing with him, I allow him to slide his arm around my waist and guide me out of the steakhouse.

CHAPTER 9
COLTON

'm still shaking with rage as I guide Ashley out of the restaurant and to my car. The mere sight of them seated together at the small two-seater table was enough to have me grinding my teeth, but hearing that cocksucker actually proposition her had me wanting to send his face through the fucking tabletop—with my fist.

"Where are we going?" she asks, her head swiveling back toward her car as I bypass it in favor of mine.

"Give me a minute," I reply through clenched teeth, opening the passenger door of my coupe to allow her entry.

I take a few calming breaths before joining her.

"Colton, you're kind of freaking me out," she says as I start the car and pull out into traffic, all without speaking. "Seriously, blink once if you're okay and twice if you're not."

At the red light, I give her two slow blinks.

"Okay." She draws out the word, her uncertainty evident. "Elaborate a little, please?"

"I told you he was a snake." The words leave my mouth on a choppy exhale.

"Yes, you did," Ashley says slowly. "What were you doing there?"

I glance at her from the side of my eye. Dressed in a white, form-sitting dress topped with a black blazer, she looks like a secretary—you know, if your secretary is sexy as hell, with candy-colored hair and pouty lips that love to sass you, so you fuck her from behind over your desk as punishment.

Hell, that exact scenario is probably what Douchebag Danny was hoping for. Over my dead fucking body.

"I was there for you."

"There for—who has stalking tendencies now, Mr. Banks?"

I offer her a tight grin. "Call me Colton."

Ashley tips her head back and laughs, the sound soft and lilting. "How generous of you."

"Smartass." I drive us toward the city limits, feeling lighter than I have in a long, long time.

As we move further away from Cottonwood, the scenery changes, going from stately homes and mani-cured lawns to boarded-up shotgun houses and dry, weed-choked grass. "Where are we going?" she asks again.

I pull off the road and park along the curb. "You see that house?" I ask, tipping my chin toward a little hovel with peeling blue paint, a busted-out-and-tarped front window and leaning front steps.

"What about it?"

"That's where I grew up."

She doesn't reply right away, but the widening of her eyes betrays her thoughts.

After a considerable pause, she asks, "Why are you showing me this?"

I drum my fingers on my plush, leather-wrapped steering wheel. "You were right—we got off on the wrong foot. This is me…trying to make amends."

"Not that I'm unappreciative, but how does bringing me here do that?"

I was hoping she'd get it without me having to spell it out. Foolish, because luck has never been on my side. Just like I had to crawl my way out of poverty, I'm going to have to fight tooth and nail to get Ashley to see me as anything other than heartless.

The question is when did I start caring about how she sees me—and why?

"Most people, you included, see me as an asshole. Arrogant. Cruel." I force a humorless laugh. "Hell, I am those things. But I'm more, too. I'm the son of two blue-collar mothers who worked five jobs combined to keep that shitty roof over our heads and cheap-ass food on the table. I'm the first in a long line to obtain a high school diploma, much less a Juris Doctor in law. People see my nice car and my expensive suits and assume I was born with a silver spoon in my mouth. But I wasn't. If anything, I was born with a chip on my shoulder. I busted ass for everything I have. And, yeah, I'm more than a little jaded, but—"

Ashley's small hand enveloping my larger one silences me mid-sentence. "Colton, I've always known you're more than the mask you wear."

"Oh, yeah? And how's that? Did a little birdie tell you?"

She chuckles. "It's like you have an asshole reflex."

I flip my hand beneath hers so we're palm-to-palm

before interlacing our fingers. "Pretty much. Would you believe me if I said I'll work on it?"

"Not even a little."

"Fair enough." I give her hand a squeeze before letting go and putting my M8 back into gear.

"Do your moms still live here?"

"Not in that hovel. They have a house here, but spend most of their time in Dogwood, at their beach house."

"Ooh, fancy," she sighs wistfully. "A beach house sounds nice."

We both fall silent after that, until halfway back, when Ashley's stomach rumbles loudly, reminding us both that she missed her lunch. "You wanna grab something to eat?"

She glances at the clock on my dash and then back to me. "I would, but I have a lot of editing to do. And I need to find a lawyer."

"Let me represent you. Please, Ashley. I'll even cut you a deal on my fees."

She nibbles her lower lip, contemplating my offer. "Fine," she concedes, "but no discount."

I pull my car into a spot a few down from where she's parked. "Stubborn woman. I'll email over the contract. Look it over, let me know. If everything looks good, drop it off at my office?"

"Oh, I'm allowed to drop by now?"

"Ha-ha, funny girl."

She shoots a saucy wink my way before climbing out of my car. My eyes remain glued to her as she walks toward her Subaru, only dipping down to her firm ass and long legs twice.

CHAPTER 10
ASHLEY

I decide to take Colton at his word and drop by the following day with the signed copy of his contract.

However, I also have a tray of cupcakes I baked last night before bed, to temper his asshole reflex.

When I walk into his office, he's in the middle of a phone call. He's using his lawyer voice, and I'm not going to lie, the commanding tone is making my panties a little wet.

"Unacceptable. Absolutely unacceptable." He quiets as the person on the line has their say. His frustration is evident in the furrow of his brow and the staccato rhythm he's beating out with his pen against the wood of his desk.

"The answer was no the first time, it is no this time, and it will be no every time you ask in the future. You know our terms, and we're unwilling to move on this." More silence ensues, followed by, "Then I guess we've said all we need to say."

Colton ends the call and shifts his attention to me. "Ashley."

"Sorry to barge in," I say, lifting my right shoulder in a semi-shrug as I test the waters of our newly forged friendship.

He waves his hand dismissively. "No worries. That call was inconsequential. What brings you by?"

I set the confection-housing-container down onto the coffee table and slide the contract from my purse. "Wanted to give you these."

He takes the papers from my outstretched hand, quickly scanning the pages. "Glad to see you came to your senses."

"You sure are packing a lot of ego, Mr. Banks." My focus dips below his belt; *I wonder what he's packing there?* I slowly bring my gaze back to his. His pants and button down cling to his lean, muscular physique. *Good glob.* If the rest of him is anything to go off of, I bet he's huge.

His cornflower eyes darken to navy pools, as if he heard my dirty thoughts.

"What's that?" he asks, nodding toward the coffee table.

"Cupcakes."

He nods. "Still plying me with sweets?"

I pivot around and bend to retrieve the tray. As I turn to face him, his eyes fly back up to mine. Deciding to call him on it, I ask, "Were you checking out my ass?"

Colton's cheeks pinken as he clears his throat. "Figured I'd repay the favor."

"Touché." I pop the lid off and pass him a cupcake.

A sense of deep satisfaction fills me as he bites into it and groans his appreciation. "Fuck, this is delicious. What is it?"

"A cupcake." I grin, knowing my reply will annoy him.

"The flavor, Ashley."

"You're too easy." I nudge his shoulder with mine before grabbing a sweet treat for myself. "It's strawberry with a strawberry white chocolate buttercream."

"This is better than the muffins," he mumbles around a bite.

I quirk a brow. "Oh, so you ate them? Interesting."

He pops the last bite into his mouth. "Don't let it go to your head."

"I don't know, that seems like a high praise from the likes of you." I do my best to look demure, twirling a strand of hair around my index finger as I bat my long, sooty lashes. "In fact, I think it's the nicest thing you've ever said to me."

"That smart mouth of yours—" His eyes drop to my lips as he speaks the words.

He steps closer to me, and my heart pitter-patters hard and fast beneath my breastbone. He leans in, a fraction of an inch, but it's enough to have my breath sawing in and out of my lungs.

My skin turns to gooseflesh as Colton lifts his hand to cup my cheek, his thumb swiping over my lower lip. "You got a little frosting…" The rumble of his voice has my core pulsing with need.

And when he pops his thumb into his mouth and sucks the buttercream off, my ovaries pretty much explode, imagining it's my cream he's sucking from his fingers instead.

"Um. Thanks." My voice is breathy as I step back from him, hoping like hell a little distance will calm my out of control libido.

"Right." Colton retreats behind his desk to the relative safety of his leather swivel chair. "Why don't you have a seat and we can talk about what's going on."

Like a switch has been flipped, he's all business.

His mood swings are faster than my damn shutter speed. Nevertheless, I lower myself into the chair in front of his desk and launch into an explanation of the nightmare that landed me in this very office a month ago.

The entire time I'm speaking, Colton remains as stoic as ever. "I need you to send me a copy of your contract with her, as well as the images. Can you do that?"

"Is a link to a viewing gallery acceptable?"

"More than. Once I look over everything, I'll give you a call." He turns to his computer screen, clearly finished with me.

His easy dismissal stings, but I shouldn't be surprised. It's Colton, after all, and it seems our newly forged friendship comes with a learning curve—or maybe it's a minefield.

CHAPTER 11
COLTON

houghts of Ashley have plagued me since our near-kiss last week. I wanted to kiss her; hell, I nearly did. It was pure luck she had icing clinging to her lower lip, providing me the perfect alibi.

While I wasn't lying to her when I said she wasn't my type, it seems perhaps my type is changing, because suddenly all I can think of is tangling my fingers in her lavender hair and feeling her long, slender legs wrapped around me. She's become almost an obsession, which is unacceptable. Not to mention, unethical. From the minute Ashley signed her name on the dotted line, she became strictly off-limits.

I've never acted inappropriately with a client before, and I don't plan to start now. However, what happens in the privacy of my own home between myself, my hand, and my very vivid imagination is fair game.

And imagine her I do as I stroke myself languidly—only in my mind, it's her small hand wrapped tightly around my rigid cock. She pumps me once, twice, three times before leaning forward and closing her lips around the crown.

She hollows her cheeks, sucking me like it's her God-given duty. I quicken my pace and envision her staring up at me with those green eyes of hers. "I wanna taste you, Colton." She practically moans the words, as if the thought of getting me off gets her off.

I'm all too happy to oblige. I clutch the sheets as my hips buck, fucking my hand the way I'd like to do her pouty pink lips, until my release spills hotly across my abdomen.

Feeling calmer after my release, I soap up and rinse off in the shower before collapsing into my bed. As expected, I fall asleep to thoughts of her.

An indiscernible amount of time later, a loud noise wakes me. It takes a second for me to realize it's the sound of someone knocking on my door. "Who the fuck?" I mumble, bleary-eyed and half asleep. I stomp down the hall toward the incessant banging, ready to tear a new one to the asshole playing my door like a drum at three o'clock in the morning.

"What?" I snarl as I fling the door open, bringing me face-to-face with someone I was sure I'd never see again—my old college flame, Kelsey Langmore. Shock at seeing her renders me speechless. It's been nearly seven years since I last saw her.

If I'm being honest, she looks like hell. She's rail thin, with gaunt cheeks. Her once-vibrant eyes are lifeless and her skin dull. "Long time no talk," she rasps coolly, like we're old friends instead of former lovers who crashed and burned in a raging dumpster fire of destruction.

"What are you doing here?" I ask, my voice even. Our relationship was the very definition of toxic. We both sought out every string of insecurity in the other and tugged until it unraveled. We partied nightly. I was failing my classes and almost lost my scholarship.

I'll never forget waking up in a random frat-house bedroom, butt-ass naked, sandwiched between Kelsey and her best friend, with no memory of our night together.

I worked too damn hard to get out of the shit-hole I grew up in to risk going back. I knew then and there, something had to change.

She agreed—or so I thought—only while I was busy trying to get back on the right path, she was out partying it up.

Getting my shit together was hard, really hard. But I managed. I even scored an internship. We clawed our way back from the depths of college-party hell. I thought Kelsey did, too, right up until she vanished, leaving only a note.

I haven't seen or heard from her since. *Until now.*

She steps to the side, revealing a young boy. He's a tall, gangly thing, with golden blond hair and pool-blue eyes. My heart races as bile creeps up my esophagus. Because looking at this kid is tantamount to looking at one of my childhood photographs.

"This is Cruz," she says, pushing him toward me ever so slightly. His clothes are stained—his cheeks are, too, with what looks like a mixture of dirt and tears. My heart aches for him, and I've only just learned his name.

"And he is?" I ask, needing to hear her actually say it.

"Your son." She spits the words, her tone lacking all maternal affection.

"I see." Questions race through my brain, rapid fire. *Where has she been the last seven years? Why did she hide my son's existence from me? Is he really mine?* Judging from the fact that he is my exact replica, I'm pretty sure I know the answer to that, but any lawyer worth his salt knows that DNA is king. *Why are they here now?*

"Could we...could we stay the night?" She shifts on her feet as she scratches at her collarbone. "I'll be out of your hair before sun up."

Every shred of good sense I possess is shouting at me to say no, all-caps yelling at me that this is a terrible idea. Hell, I wouldn't be surprised if she robbed me, judging by the way she keeps straining to see into my condo.

But there's no way I'm turning my son away, especially when his mother looks so strung out. I know this is most likely a monumental mistake, and still, I push the door open wider and invite them in.

***

The following morning, I wake earlier than usual, despite my nighttime disturbance. A million and one different emotions are rioting through my body—the biggest of all, regret for not speaking a single word to my son upon meeting him last night.

Though, it wasn't much of a meeting, was it? Regardless, I could have done more. Made a bigger effort. Instead, I acted like he wasn't there.

Chalking it up to shock, I vow to make up for it today. Right after I shower. And maybe have some coffee, too.

Thirty minutes later, I step into the hallway dressed and ready. I'm wearing my lucky suit—never lost a case in it. My face is freshly shaved and my hair gelled. In short, I'm ready for battle. And by battle, I mean to meet my son and grill Kelsey about where the fuck she's been the last seven years.

Only, when I step out into the living room, Cruz is all alone. "Where's your mom?" I ask. But he doesn't reply.

"Cruz, where is your mom?" I come around to the front of the couch.

Still, nothing.

"Listen, kid, I need to know where your mom is. Can you help me out?"

With small movements, he nudges an envelope across the couch cushion toward me. Leaning down, I grab it and run my finger beneath the flap. Inside is a single sheet of paper folded in half. I slide the page out and read it.

Colton,

Yes, he's yours. I left after finding out I was pregnant. I planned on aborting the kid, but…fuck, I don't know. Call it a crisis of conscience. Whatever it was, I couldn't do it.

I'm sure you're reading this and judging me. But I'm not cut out to be a mom. I tried, but it's just not for me. He doesn't talk, or won't talk. I don't really know. But I'm done. It's your turn now.

All of his important shit (birth certificate, social secu-
rity card, etc.) is in his bag.
    -Kelsey

Another fucking note—only this time, instead of leaving me,
she left…my kid.

"Fuck!" I shout, before I think better of it.

I spin to Cruz. My throat constricts at the sight of him folded in on himself, with his knees to his chest and his forehead pressed to his knees.

Great. Now he's probably scared of me. "I-I'm sorry for yelling," I tell him, scrubbing a hand over my face as I sway on my feet before collapsing down onto the couch beside my son.

He shrugs. *At least I know he can understand me.*

"Can you talk?" I ask, hoping for…I don't even know what.

Again, he shrugs. I sigh.

"Are you hungry?"

A nod.

"Okay, then." I head into the kitchen, wishing like hell I had some of those chocolate chip cheesecake muffins to offer him instead of oatmeal and eggs.

Shit. Does he have any allergies? I turn around and stride back into the living room to retrieve his bag.

His one, single bag. This woman dropped him off with one meager bag. I dump it, cataloging the contents: one pair of pants, two pairs of underwear, a shirt, a single pair of mismatched socks, and all of his important paperwork shoved into a sandwich bag.

Anger like nothing I've ever known courses through me, but I suppress it. My outburst earlier scared Cruz, and there's no way in hell I'm having my son fear me.

As I sort through the papers, I don't see anything mentioning allergies, but seeing as his mother dropped him off with a virtual stranger—father or not—I don't exactly trust her maternal instincts.

"Second thought, let's go out. We'll get breakfast on the way…" My words trail off as I realize he'll have to come to work with me. "Let me just make a phone call, okay?"

He nods, still seated where I found him this morning.

I retreat to my bedroom and dial West. "What?" he grumbles into the phone, his voice still weighted with sleep.

"I need your help."

There's rustling and then, "At six in the morning?"

"6:05, actually."

"Colton!" he growls.

"Listen, man, I wouldn't ask if it wasn't important. Kelsey turned up here at like three in the morning—"

"Kelsey…like the Kelsey who almost destroyed your life?"

"That's dramatic. I'm as much to blame, but, yes. Her."

"Why?" he asks, suddenly awake and alert.

"If you'd stop interrupting, you'd know." I pause, wanting to make sure West is ready to listen, because repeating myself is not something I enjoy on a good day, and this is decidedly not a good day. "Anyway, she showed up last night with her kid. *My* kid."

West chokes. "I'm sorry, did you say *your* kid?"

"Yes. My son. His name is Cruz."

"And he's yours?"

I pinch the bridge of my nose. "That's what I said. Look, can you meet me at my office?"

"Sure, man."

"Great. Wait! Do five year olds need a car seat or anything?" I ask, cringing at just how unprepared I am to be a father.

"It depends on his height and weight. Most likely he should be in a booster with a five-point harness."

"Fuck."

"Take a breath, man. Are you sure she didn't leave one?"

"I don't see one anywhere. Just a duffel bag. And you, know, a kid."

"Look around."

Humoring him, I walk back into the living room. Cruz is still on the couch where I left him, staring at the wall. "Hang on, West."

I grab the Fire remote from the hearth and hand it to Cruz. "You like TV?" He nods. "I've got Netflix, Prime, and Hulu. Watch whatever you want…well, you know…something appropriate."

West chuckles. "Good parenting talk, man."

"Shut up," I grumble, resuming my search. "I don't see it anywhere."

"Check the hall."

"I just said I didn't see it anywhere. I would definitely see a car seat in my hallway."

"The outside hall, idiot."

I open my front door and sure enough, tucked against the façade of my condo, is a booster seat that looks like it's seen better days. "Good call. Any idea how to put this fucker in my car?"

"YouTube is your friend. Watch a video or two and you'll have it in no time."

We hang up, with the promise to meet at my office in an hour. Which means I only have a few minutes to figure out how to install this thing and get out the door.

CHAPTER 12
ASHLEY

"How are things?" Mally asks, her voice a comfort, even through the phone.

"Meh."

"Ash, I need more than meh. Talk to me."

"I don't know. Things are…things."

My best friend huffs. "Start talking or I'll drive my pregnant ass back to Mississippi—"

"You realize that's incentive for me not to talk, right?"

"Ashley!"

I click around on my computer, pulling up my business's Facebook page. There are hundreds of notifications—all for comments from Megan Grace and her bitch brigade, no doubt. I also have twenty new ratings, all 1-star, along with a slew of messages mean enough to make Draco Malfoy cry.

"Hard, things are hard. I can pretty much feel my dream slipping away, all because of one batshit bride. I am lusting after my lawyer and stress baking daily."

"I've been following the comments. Reporting them,

too. Pretty sure she's a witch, though, because for every comment I report, four new ones pop up."

"Oh, she's definitely a witch—with a capital B."

"Has Mister Hot Lawyer made any progress?"

I groan. "I have to meet him in an hour, actually. I sent over her image gallery, along with our contract and screenshots, on Wednesday."

"Hmm. Maybe you'll get to start the weekend with good news."

Mallory's hopefulness bolsters my own. "Maybe."

"Shoot! I gotta go, Duke just walked in the door with lunch."

"Tell Officer Kincaid hello for me."

"Will do. Love you big!"

"Love you bigger," I say, ending the call.

I park a block away from Colton's office, planning to hit up Bru on my way over for an iced vanilla-lavender latte. At the last minute, I grab him a coffee, too. He always drinks it plain at his office, but with his sweet tooth, I decide to take a chance and order him a Milky Way latte.

With both beverages in hand, I set off for his office, hope and terror clashing within my chest. If he has anything other than good news for me…

No! I suck down a sip of my drink and squash that train of thought. Negativity begets negativity, and I'm *positive* I'm in the right. I refuse to even entertain the notion that Megan Grace is going to best me.

"I brought coff—" My words hit a wall when I walk in to find a young boy in ill-fitting clothes sitting on the couch in the waiting area, with no adults in sight. He looks no older than five or six, has golden skin, blue eyes, and hair the color of caramel. "Hey there, what's your name?"

He looks up at me, mild interest sparking in his gaze, but he doesn't tell me his name.

I deposit our drinks on the table and take a seat in the chair across from him. "Are you here with your mom or dad?"

His nod is nearly imperceptible.

Colton's meeting before me must have run over. "Have you been waiting here for a long time?" I ask.

Another nod.

This poor kid has to be bored out of his mind. There's not a single thing in this waiting area to entertain him. You know, unless children enjoy law books and Time Magazine.

"Would you like to play a game on my phone?"

He shakes his head.

"What about books—do you like books?"

His blue eyes brighten.

I fish my Kindle out of my purse and pull up the store. "Do you like adventure?" I pause to watch his response between each question. "Fantasy? What about Dr. Seuss?"

He shrugs after each, so I settle on Seuss, because what kid doesn't like Dr. Seuss?

"May I sit by you?" I ask, not wanting to make the little dude feel uncomfortable.

He pats the cushion next to him with his small hand.

I situate myself on the couch and download *Green Eggs and Ham* to my Kindle.

We finish it and dive straight in to *The Lorax*, which

has the little cutie grinning and giggling. The sound of his innocent, sweet laughter has me doing the same, and all too soon we're both laughing fools.

Colton appears in the doorway, an odd look in his eyes. "What's going on out—oh, hey, you're here."

West peeks his head out from behind the blond man and my curiosity prickles. My pint-sized friend said he was here with his parents—but neither of the men before me fit the bill. *Maybe his parents are here, too?*

Ignoring the two men, my little buddy tugs on my shirt. "More," he whispers, his voice a barely audible murmur.

"Sure—"

"Did he just speak to you?" Colton asks harshly, cutting me off. The boy scoots closer to me; instinctively, I take his little hand in mine.

There's obviously far more happening here than meets the eye. "We're reading," I say firmly, as if it's answer enough.

"Ashley." Colton's long fingers wrap around the doorframe in a white-knuckle grip. "A word?"

I grin up at him. "Sure." And then down at my new friend. "Right after we read this next book." I download *Horton Hears a Who* and begin reading the heartwarming tale out loud.

From the corner of my eye, I see West shoulder past his friend and settle into the chair I vacated earlier. Colton, however, remains rooted to the spot, his stare burning a hole into the side of my face.

By the time we reach the end of the story, the little dude is nestled into my side, sleeping soundly. "What's going on?" I ask softly, as not to wake him. "Where are his parents?"

Neither man answers immediately.

West leans back in his chair, his mouth pulled into an anticipatory smirk. "Well, his mom skipped town."

Colton pinches the bridge of his nose and drops heavily into the chair beside his friend. "He's mine."

The pistons in my mind misfire. "Your what?"

"My son," Colton says, straightening in his chair, his blue eyes hard on my green.

I swallow roughly.

My soulmate has a son. For a split-second, sadness engulfs me—sadness that someone else gave him the greatest gift there is—but just as quickly a radiant burst of happiness replaces it. The universe is granting me a gift and deeming me worthy of being in this adorable kid's life. I only wonder why Colton hasn't ever mentioned his son before?

No matter the reason, I can sense there's something special about this kid. He glows with goodness, and I'll do my damn best to be whatever it is he needs me to be.

"Cool. Cool, cool. Cool." I sound like Jake Peralta from *Brooklyn Nine-Nine.* "How old is he?"

"Five."

I nod, at a loss on what else to say. It's on the tip of my tongue to ask him why he's never mentioned him before, but I swallow it down as Colton begins speaking.

"I…he…his mother dropped him off last night."

"Abandoned him is more like it," West adds.

Ever-so-carefully I pull my arm from beneath his sleeping form and wrap it around him, pulling him closer to me. "Abandoned?" The mere notion makes me ill.

"Showed up out of the blue, told Colton he was his, and left before the sun came up."

My heart feels brittle, like it's liable to break at any moment. "She what?"

Colton nods. "She left a note, and duffel bag with a change of clothes."

"Oh my glob. Poor baby."

The two imposing looking men exchange glances. "What are your plans this weekend and can you clear them?" Colton asks.

"I don't have anything going on, why?"

"Because when Cruz spoke to you…it's the only time I've heard him speak. I'm man enough to admit I'm out of my depth here, with him and fatherhood in general. So, yeah, since you're free…I could really use the help."

I hide my grin behind my hands. *I guess a man like Colton can only humble himself so far*—even when asking for help. "Of course. Anything you need," I say, meaning it. I can't even begin to imagine how either of them, father and son alike, must be feeling.

Right here in this moment, with a sleeping Cruz curled into my side and weary-eyed Colton across from me, I decide it's my mission to help the two of them wade through these uncharted and murky waters.

CHAPTER 13
COLTON

e spoke to her.

That's all I can think as I watch my son sleep, snuggled up to my purple-haired menace. *Though, she's not really a menace anymore, is she?* No, I can think of far better descriptors for Ashley Murphy—the main one right now being a lifesaver.

She's not mine either.

"Has he eaten?" Ashley asks, running her fingers through his hair.

"Uh, we grabbed breakfast on the way here about seven."

"Colton! It's almost one!" She whips her glare over to West. "Seriously? As a dad, you should know better."

"I know, we just got caught up in trying to figure out everything with Kelsey."

Ashley raises her perfectly sculpted eyebrows.

"His mother," I clarify.

"Did you find anything?"

West shakes his head, but I speak. "We found a few social media profiles, but she hasn't been active on them." My lips thin in disgust. "She didn't have a single picture of him. It was all shots of her partying."

Ashley wears a frown that rivals mine. She appears as repulsed by the whole situation as I am.

"I don't know if it would help, but my best friend's husband is a cop. Maybe he could look into it?"

I'm half tempted to take her up on it, but I shake my head in refusal. I've always kept my business on the right side of the law and don't plan to venture into murky territory now.

"What's the plan?" Ashley asks, like she has every right to know.

"Lunch?" It comes out as a question, and I hate the uncertainty ricocheting through me.

She shakes her head, causing wispy purple hairs to tickle her cheekbones. "No, big picture."

"A paternity test. Obviously, he's mine, but I'm no fool. I want irrefutable proof he's mine. I want to make sure Kelsey can't just waltz back in and take him after keeping him from me his entire life. I've also put calls out to the hospital listed on his birth certificate in hopes of medical records, and to a social worker, here locally."

West and I go to speak at the same time; I signal for him to go ahead. "You also need to set up a bedroom for him and stuff like that."

"Which means shopping," I add.

"I suppose you're both right." *Where do you take a kid to shop?*

Ashley shoots me a cheeky smile that makes my heart stutter in my chest. "I usually am. But we can do that tomorrow. Today—after he wakes up—we eat and have fun. You need to bond with him."

I start to bristle at her words, but tamper down the

urge with a rough swallow. "Right. Food, fun, and bonding."

West laughs. "Oh, how your Friday nights are about to change, my friend."

"You're confusing me for you." I shoot my friend a withering glare.

"Whatever." West waves his wedding band-clad hand through the air. "Why don't we all grab a bite together on Sunday? I know Asher is a lot younger, but maybe being around other kids will help."

"Sounds good. Text me to set it up."

West nods as he rises to his feet. "See y'all. I gotta get home to the missus."

Silence lingers for several minutes after West's departure, until Ashley asks me what kind of food Cruz likes.

Frustrated, I run a hand through my hair, tugging on the ends. "Honestly? I have no idea. How messed up is that? I have a son and don't even know his favorite food. Or his favorite color. I don't know what he's scared of or what makes him smile." My eyes sting with emotion. "I don't know him."

"You will. Give it—*him*—time." Ashley sounds so sure, so confident in me, that I almost believe her.

"What if I fuck it all up?" I ask, my voice quivering slightly. I feel vulnerable, like my chest is cracked open and Ashley can see all of my tender insides.

Before she can answer, Cruz wakes. He looks from Ashley to me and back again before sitting up and wiping the sleep from his eyes.

"You hungry?" Ashley asks with a soft voice.

Cruz nods.

"What sounds tasty?" She grins and rubs her hands

together. "Personally, I could go for a big, juicy burger. Do you like burgers?"

"Yeah," he whispers in that raspy little voice of his.

"Okay, then, burgers it is. Let me grab my keys." I stand and walk to my desk to retrieve my phone, wallet, and keys. On my way back, the sound of Cruz talking to Ashley draws me up short.

I know I shouldn't, but I stand and listen.

"Are you f-friends with…him?" he asks.

Ashley doesn't answer right away. "I am," she says finally.

"Is he nice?" His small, timid voice, coupled with his question, nearly has me doubling over in grief for him.

"He is. I can only imagine how scary this is for you. But Colton—your daddy—he's a really good man, and I can already tell he loves you very much. I know it's hard, all of this change, but I think you two will be good for each other."

"He loves me?" I rub at my breastbone, trying to soothe the ache caused by Cruz's hopeful uncertainty.

I don't know what his life has been like up until now, but going forward, I will make fucking sure that little boy knows love and kindness and safety and happiness. And God help anyone who tries to stop me.

Over the course of mammoth-sized cheeseburgers, salty fries, and milkshakes, I watch as Ashley makes my son smile over and over again. By the time we finish our lunch, I know what his laugh sounds like, and, hands down, it is the best sound I've ever heard.

"Do you like playing outside?" I ask him as we walk down the sidewalk toward my car.

He looks my way, his eyes wide. For a split-second, I

think he's going to speak to me, but he doesn't. He simply nods.

"There's a park down the street. We could…play…if you want."

Cruz nods again, this time with a half-grin.

It may not seem like much, but it's the first smile he's given me, and I feel like a million bucks.

"Great, let's go," I say, and the three of us set off down toward the park, Cruz and Ashley walking hand-in-hand with me following slightly behind, wishing like hell I could connect to him as easily as she can.

CHAPTER 14
ASHLEY

Cruz's cherubic little face lights up when the park comes into view. Three platforms of varying heights, connected by an array of bridges, monkey bars, and tunnels, jut up into the sky. There are six different slides, a few sets of swings, and a rock wall. And those are just the things I can name. This is not your basic swings, slide, merry-go-round type of kiddie park. Nope, this is the crème-de-la-crème, with all the bells and whistles—like an all-inclusive, 5-star resort-style playground. The only thing missing is a poker table and free drinks.

While I don't know the names of, much less how to use most of the equipment here, my little friend does, and he's chomping at the bit to explore them all.

"What do you want to do first?" Colton asks his son.

Cruz hesitantly points to the massive tire swing, dropping his hand as quickly as he raised it—almost as if he's expecting to be told no.

"Let's do it," Colton says, offering Cruz his hand to hold.

I watch with bated breath. For an unending second, the little boy simply stares at his father's hand, studying it like it's a complicated equation that's gone unsolved for eons.

Right as I see Colton giving up hope of his son taking his hand, Cruz interlaces their fingers. My heart hums happily in my chest as the defeat clouding Colton's eyes morphs to pure joy.

I slink away to a shaded bench as the duo head toward the tire swing, content to watch and snap cell phone pics from the sidelines as they get to know one another.

The sound of Cruz's laughter as Colton winds up the chains and sends the tire flying is the most magical thing I've ever heard. All of the women—and even a few men—notice my two guys playing, because, let's be honest, it's not every day you see a six-foot plus man hot enough to walk the runway play with his kid in the dirt and mulch while wearing a suit.

I can't fault them for drooling over him either; I'm pretty sure I've made a puddle big enough to splash in. There's something about watching him interact with his kid that ignites this deep-seated, primordial part of my brain. It's as though I have a loincloth-wearing cave-woman inside of me, shaking a bone in the air while yelling *"Mate, mate, mate!"*

I trail behind them, careful not to intrude as they transition from one play area to another. They don't speak with words while they play, instead communicating in hand gestures, nods, and smiles. If Cruz's shrieking laughter is anything to go by, they're having plenty of fun.

After a good forty minutes of playing, my boys—*I*

mean the *boys*—join me beneath the shade of a massive oak tree. "Are you having fun?" I ask Cruz.

"Yes," is his whispered reply. I'm not sure why he deems me worthy of his precious, raspy words, but it's a blessing I readily accept.

"Have you played on everything you wanted to?"

He scans the park a few times, his gaze pausing on the slides every time.

"You want to slide?" I ask.

He nods.

"Go for it, dude!"

Cruz turns to his father with pleading blue eyes.

"What's up, bud?" Colton asks.

His mini-me tugs on his belt loop, his blond head canting toward the slides.

"I think he wants you to slide with him."

Colton looks to the dirt-dusted slide with the muddy mulch puddle at the bottom and then down at his son. His internal battle plays out in his every feature, from his lowered brow to his thinned lips.

I don't fret though; I know he'll make the right choice —that'll he slide down that dirty slide, expensive suit be damned, because his son feeling safe, secure, and loved is far more important than any potential dry-cleaning bill.

"Let's do it!" Colton takes Cruz's hand and together they set off for the slides.

I happily snap picture after picture of my boys as they exit the chutes and tubes, capping the gallery off with a frame-worthy shot of them racing down the side-by-side slide hand-in-hand.

We cap off our playground adventure with snoballs and glass bottle sodas from a little food cart in front of the park before walking the few blocks back to Colton's office.

"Do you have plans for dinner?" Colton asks as we near the purple door marking his building.

"I do not. Unless you count vegging out with some ramen on the couch while binging Netflix plans."

He bites his lips and raises his brows, a boyish combo if there ever was one. "Wanna veg out with ramen at my place instead?" He discreetly tips his head toward Cruz.

"Sure, sounds good. Text me the address?"

"Will do." He leans in as if he's going to hug me, making my lungs seize and my heart stutter.

Subconsciously, I sway toward him, anxious to know how his strong arms feel around me. Only, it never happens.

Instead, he tucks my hair behind my ear and whispers, "Thank you for your help today, with Cruz."

You fool! Of course, he wasn't going to hug you. Get a grip! "Yeah, sure. Anytime." My tongue darts out to moisten my lips and for a split-second, I swear his eyes dip down and follow the movement. *Wishful thinking,* my brain taunts.

Before I can make a total fool of myself, I redirect my attention to Cruz. "I'll see you in a few minutes, okay?"

The little boy fidgets with the hem of his shirt. "Promise?" His voice is barely audible.

I drop down to my knees so we're eye level and draw an X over my heart with my index finger. "Cross my heart promise."

He cocks his head to the side in question.

"It's like a pinky promise, but stronger. Unbreakable."

He studies me intently, searching for signs of deception. I don't know much of anything about this boy's life, but it's clear to me he's been let down time and time again by adults who should have cared for and protected him. I have no intention of joining the list of people who have failed this sweet boy. If anything, I'm going to see to it that he thrives.

"Okay," he says eventually, wrapping his lanky arms around my shoulders.

CHAPTER 15
COLTON

From the minute we arrived back at my place, Cruz has been parked on the couch, watching the door like a hawk as he waits for Ashley to show up.

"She'll be here soon, bud," I tell him after fifteen minutes have come and gone.

My son looks at me with big, pleading eyes as he worries his lip.

The hopeful devastation on Cruz's face hits me like an uppercut to my kidneys. Ashley promised him she'd be here and is nowhere to be found. I grab a seat beside him and shoot her a text. No answer.

Another five minutes pass and his blue eyes resemble glassy pools. Credit where it's due, the kid doesn't let a single tear fall.

Which only serves to knock me down a little more, because how much disappointment does a five-year-old have to have faced in his life to not cry when someone breaks a promise?

Then again, he didn't cry when Kelsey abandoned him here either. *Fuck. That's probably not normal.*

Furious and unbelieving, I call Ashley, but it goes straight to voice mail.

Once we hit twenty-five minutes, I decide to call it. "I'm sorry, Cruz. Maybe we can watch a movie and—"

The sound of knocking cuts me off.

Cruz and I both bolt up from the couch and race to the door. Sure enough, my purple-haired menace is on the other side, both arms laden down with grocery bags.

"So sorry! I had an idea we could make homemade pizzas and some cupcakes. I went to text you when I got to the store, but my phone was dead." She turns to Cruz. "Do you forgive me?"

He replies with a question of his own. "What kind?"

"Oh, the cupcakes?"

My son nods—seems like he has my sweet tooth.

"I was thinking we could do dirt cupcakes."

Cruz's button nose crinkles in disgust.

"Not real dirt, silly boy. We'll crush Oreo cookies!"

His eyes go wide as he nods frantically. *Definitely has my sweet tooth.*

In the kitchen, Ashley rolls out the pizza dough before helping Cruz spread the sauce. We each have a third of the pizza and top it accordingly—pepperoni, mushrooms, and peppers for me, spinach, tomatoes, bacon, and hot sauce for Ashley, and plain pepperoni for Cruz.

While it bakes, they work on the cupcake batter and icing mixture.

"You wanna help?" Ashley asks, whisking quickly.

I lean back against the edge of the counter, smirking. "For as much as I love sweets, a baker I am not."

"Taste tester, then," she chirps back, nudging Cruz with her elbow.

"Fine by me. I'm going to look over a few emails. Let me know when my services are needed."

At the island, I scroll through all of the documents Ashley sent me in regard to the bride who has been terrorizing her. The contract between the two of them clearly states the terms, and the screenshots of the emails between them clearly show Ashley tried rescheduling the portrait session. It's fairly cut and dry—to me, at least—that this bride is nothing more than a spoiled little dolt out to score something for nothing, not caring a single iota who she hurts along the way.

A shadow falls over my laptop keyboard. "Taste this, please?"

I take the icing-filled spoon and wrap my lips around it, groaning in delight as the deep chocolatey flavor coats my mouth. "Delicious."

Cruz grins and bounces on his toes.

"Told ya," she tells him, ruffling his hair. "He did all the mixing, and I said it was perfect, but he wanted taste-tester-dad's opinion."

I smile warmly at my son. "Best icing I've ever had."

His grin morphs to a cheek-splitting smile that I feel soul deep.

"How long until the—" A timer goes off, both interrupting me and answering my question.

Ashley makes quick work of pulling out the bubbling, cheesy pizza and popping the cupcake pan in.

We eat our pizza at the island with lemonade she bought at the store, alternating between asking Cruz questions. He answers Ashley with softly spoken words, but only gives me head shakes and nods.

But in just a day, his smiles come easier and his eyes look lighter, so I'll count it as a win all the same.

I go back to working—this time relegated to the living room—while the two of them decorate the cupcakes. I've made it through my third look-through of everything Ashley emailed over when they call me back.

"These look great!" I rub my hands together in anticipation of digging into one of the gummy-worm topped dirt cupcakes.

Ashley plates us up one each, along with a glass of milk, and we dig in. "Oh, shit, that's good."

Cruz snickers.

"Language!" Ashley reprimands, causing me to blush and my son to full-on belly laugh. *Who knew the way to a kid's heart was sweets and a good scolding?*

After we devour our sweet treats, we retreat to the couch. Cruz sits between us, snuggled into Ashley's side while we watch a show of his choosing—some cartoon about the crazy antics of two genius brothers and how they spend their 101 days of summer vacation.

Two episodes in and Cruz is out like a light, softly snoring, with his head in Ashley's lap.

"Let me move him to his bed," I say as I stand.

"Sure."

I gently lift him and carry him down the hall to the guest room—well, his room now. He looks so small in the middle of the queen-sized bed. One thing's for sure, though: this room, while nicely decorated in soothing grays and whites, is in no way suited to a kid.

Back in the living room, Ashley is packing her stuff up. "Wait!" I whisper-shout, panicking at the thought of her leaving, at the thought of being solely in charge of Cruz's safety and well-being overnight. "Stay."

"Stay?" she parrots back. "Why?"

Sweat beads my brow as I search for a reason that will entice her to stick around. "We need to talk about your problem bride."

"Shouldn't that happen during…like…office hours?"

I smirk, downplaying my sudden nerves. "That's cute."

Somehow, she sees through my act. "Colton, what's this really about?"

I deflate and drop down onto the couch, hanging my head. "What if Cruz has a bad dream or something? What if he gets scared or cries for Kelsey? You're the only person he speaks to. So, please, stay?"

CHAPTER 16
ASHLEY

The butterflies in my belly flap their wings, telling me that agreeing to stay is a mistake, but the thought of that sweet little boy waking up scared and confused has me agreeing anyway. "Okay. For Cruz."

"For Cruz." His easy agreement feels like a cop-out, but I don't say anything. "But we can talk about your business situation, too."

"Okay, lawyer man, let's talk."

"Take a seat." He nods to the couch. "I'll grab my laptop."

I balance myself on the edge of the left cushion, yawning as I wait. He returns moments later, claiming the right cushion for himself, leaving the center open.

"I've read your contract, multiple times, and the terms were clear. You also made several attempts to reschedule due to the weather." He looks over to me, and the warmth in his blue eyes makes my breaths come a little faster. "Simply put, she doesn't have a leg to stand on."

I nibble the side of my lower lip. "What do we do?"

"Hopefully a cease and desist is all you'll need."

"What if it doesn't work?"

"We sue."

I fidget in my seat, anxiety rippling through me.

"You okay?" Colton asks, taking note of my discomfort.

"I, uh, I hope it doesn't come to that." I scooch a little closer to him. "We couldn't just send a second letter?"

"I mean, we could, but if she ignores the first, what's stopping her from ignoring subsequent letters? I'm good at my job, Ashley—let me do it."

"Yeah, okay." I don't fight him on it—he's right, after all. He's a professional, a well-respected one at that. Arguing with him about this would be like him telling me the best way to retouch photos.

"Let me type something up to get us going."

He opens a Word document and begins clacking away. His fingers fly over the keys like lightning, and his face is set in a mask of concentration. While he's distracted, I study him unabashedly. Colton Banks truly is a work of art—and one day, he'll be all mine.

"Okay," he says, bringing me back to earth. "Come take a look."

I slide over until we're thigh to thigh and read over what he's typed out. The tone is stern, the intent clear, and the language precise. I know if I was ever the recipient of a letter like this, I'd knock off whatever antics caused it, that's for sure.

Without thinking, I place my hand on his leg. "Thank you."

Colton's eyes drop down to where my palm is pressed into his firm, muscular thigh. "Ashley." He says my name like a warning and a prayer all wrapped up in one.

"Yeah?" My voice is a breathy whisper as I lean in a little more, close enough to smell the mouthwatering fragrance of his cologne. It's a woodsy scent with a hint of citrus, sensual and fresh and so very Colton.

He stares at me intently before diving for my lips. For a moment, I don't move, and I don't reciprocate his kiss. I'm frozen, possibly in shock. Because Colton Banks is kissing me. *Oh my glob! Colton is kissing me!*

My rational thought kicks back in, and I move my hands to his chest to shove him away, to ask him what on earth possessed him to kiss me, when he's made it abundantly clear he's not into me like that. However, it seems my libido has hijacked my brain, because instead, I find myself wrapping my fingers around his tie and pulling him closer.

Taking this as an invitation to deepen our kiss, he flicks his tongue across the seam of my lips, demanding entry. My own lips part on a moan, and Colton licks into my mouth, intent on devouring me.

My free hand finds its way into the hair at the nape of his neck. And somehow, I'm straddling his lap, with his strong, warm palms gripping my ass as he grinds himself into me. This kiss—*our first kiss*—may as well be an out of body experience, because my consciousness is merely a passenger on this lust-fueled ride.

By the time we break apart, we're both panting, and my panties are so wet I wouldn't be surprised to see a damp spot on the crotch of his pants.

"Fuck!" Colton all but shoves me from his lap. "Fuck!"

With my body mourning the loss of his and my head

swirling from his sudden rejection, confusion covers me like a heavy blanket. "What—what was that?"

His face is screwed up in an impassively blank mask that gives nothing away. He stands from the couch and straightens his tie. "A mistake."

My eyes water and my jaw nearly comes unhinged as it hangs open in disbelief. "Excuse me?"

"Kissing you was a mistake." He runs his hands through his messy hair. "My apologies."

"Are you seriously fucking apologizing for kissing me?" I ball my hands into tight fists to keep from slapping him.

"I'm just not interested in you that way."

I snort derisively as I gesture toward his tented slacks. "Your dick says differently."

He swallows roughly. "Any red-blooded man would get hard with a firm ass rubbing all over his lap. Trust me, it has nothing to do with you."

Rage courses through me as I take in the man before me. The man I know I'm destined for. The man I thought was my friend. "You have some nerve!" I shove at his broad chest.

It's like hitting a mountain made of muscle and flesh and bone.

"You don't understand," he grits out.

"Then explain it. Make me understand why you run so damn hot and cold. Why you kiss me like that then tell me I'm just a warm body!"

"Argh! You make me fucking crazy!" His voice is a quiet roar.

"Welcome to the club! You're not exactly Mr. Sunshine!"

"I'm a realist, Ashley, and in no way do we work in

the real world." He runs his eyes over my body in a way that has my shoulders bunching and my belly churning.

"What's that supposed to mean?"

He rolls his eyes, and I swear my ovaries flutter. *Stupid, traitorous reproductive system.* I don't care how damn good he looks with his sex hair and kiss-swollen lips in his rumpled suit—he's still a jackass, with the manners of a caveman and the attitude of a toddler.

"What it means," he sneers, "is you're you...and I'm me. We're simply not compatible, Ashley."

My soulmate just told me we aren't compatible. Just going to file that sickening feeling away in a folder labeled: Things that hurt worse than dropping a bowling ball on your foot.

"Great. Wonderful." I throw my arms up in the air. "Just gonna give you a bit of advice, okay? In the future, when a woman is interested in you, and you don't feel the same, maybe don't fucking kiss her, okay? Because, newsflash, asshole—it's not very nice to play with people's emotions! In fact, it's downright rotten."

A look of hurt crosses his face, but is gone in an instant. "It won't happen again."

"Glad to hear it. Now, if you don't mind, I'd like to go to bed." Colton looks at me as if I've lost my mind. And maybe I have, but...

"You asked me to stay in case you needed help with Cruz. I'm here for him. Once he's up, I'll be on my way. I know my place now."

"Ashley—"

I ignore the sorrowful lilt to his voice. "Come Monday, you can send the cease and desist to Megan Grace and shoot me an invoice via email."

CHAPTER 17
COLTON

egret and longing weigh me down as I turn and stalk down the hall toward my room. For a few glorious moments, I had my hands and mouth all over Ashley. Even now, the taste of her kiss lingers, the sweet flavor of her tempting me to turn back and beg for another taste.

But I don't—I can't. Starting anything with her while she's my client is highly unethical, regardless of how good her lean, lithe body feels beneath my palms.

I pause at the threshold to my room. "Blanket's in the hall closet," I call over my shoulder before pulling the door shut behind me.

I pace and prowl in the open space at the foot of my bed, far too wound up to go to sleep. How is it possible for my life to change so drastically in the span of a single day—for me to go from an untethered bachelor with no plans of settling down anytime soon to a single dad planning park dates while lusting after the only person his son will speak to?

It's like I woke up in an alternate universe and I'm

trapped here, with no way home in sight. That's the only possible explanation for how Ashley Murphy has managed to work herself so far beneath my skin that she's in my blood, occupying far too many of my thoughts as she races steadily from my heart to my brain then back again.

After nearly wearing a trail in my plush rug, I give up my pacing in favor of counting sheep. I only make it to fifty before sleep claims me. And no surprise, all my dreams are of her.

It's still dark when my alarm clock beeps me awake. The temptation to hit snooze is strong, but I want to be up before Cruz. Not to mention, I slept for shit anyway, thanks to a certain lavender-haired beauty plaguing my dreams—*a menace even in slumber.*

I make quick work of my morning routine, starting with a series of stretches—double reps to make up for missing them yesterday—to get my blood flowing, before hopping in the shower and dressing for the day.

Venturing into the hall, I expect stillness and silence. Imagine my surprise when I find Ashley and Cruz hard at work making… "Are those pancakes?"

Ashley nods. "Coffee's brewed."

I linger on the fringe of the open space, watching her as she methodically cranks out pancake after pancake. To the untrained eye, her softly spoken words, delivered with a pleasant smile, give an unaffected appearance, like last night never happened. But the slight tremor in her hands and the tightness in her eyes gives her away. She's still upset with me—not that I blame her.

Kissing her was bad form on my part; and yet, I can't bring myself to regret it.

I shuffle past them toward the coffee pot, wondering why they're up before the sun and in my kitchen churning out pancakes like a diner kitchen on a Sunday morning.

"Blueberries, bananas, or chocolate chips?" she asks without ever looking my way.

Cruz's eyes ping-pong between us. My quiet guy can sense the tension, and I'm desperate to put him at ease. "What do you recommend, bud?"

A small but genuine smile lights up his face as he points to the bananas, and then to the chocolate chips.

"Both, huh?"

He nods, bobblehead style.

"Sounds good." I take a sip of my steaming coffee. "Load me up."

A barely perceptible nod is the only indication Ashley heard me.

"Can I help with anything?" I'm desperate to regain the ground we covered, for us to be friends—even if the thoughts I have about her are more than friendly.

It's not just her connection with Cruz that has me scrambling to smooth things over, either. In all truth, the idea of us reverting back to enemies makes me feel a little ill.

"We got it." She softens her terse reply by bumping her shoulder against Cruz's, sending a toothy smile his way.

"Right. Okay, then. I guess I'll—"

"Just do whatever you'd usually do on a Saturday morning."

While Ashley's dismissal stings, I know it's deserved

—Lord knows I've dismissed her too many times to count now.

I settle down at the island and fire up my laptop, starting with my emails before moving on to some brain games. In what feels like no time at all, Ashley is telling me the food is ready.

We eat in the dining room instead of at the island, with Ashley and Cruz on one side of the table and me on the other. "What's the plan for today?" she asks around a bite of pancake.

I'm shocked she's sticking around to help after the way things ended last night. It speaks a lot to her character, which I am realizing more and more I sorely misjudged.

"We need to set up a bedroom for him, and he needs more clothes and toys. Thank God it's summer, so I have time to figure out school, but maybe some books." I look to my son and ask, "Do you like reading?"

He nods.

"So yeah, we pretty much need it all. I know a social worker is going to do a home study, and I want to make it abundantly clear that my son is safe here." *And nurtured and loved and wanted—so very fucking wanted.*

It's crazy how the universe works; if you'd have asked me two days ago if I ever wanted kids, I'd have told you no. And now, after meeting my son, the answer is emphatically yes. Obviously, fatherhood—single, at that—is a huge undertaking. But this kid, he's special. To an outsider, it probably seems like I'm taking this earth-shattering change a little too well, but bullshit aside, Cruz feels like my missing piece come home.

"Okay," Ashley says slowly. "It's a lot, but we can do it. After I clean up the kitchen—"

"There's no way you're cleaning after cooking two incredible meals for us. Cruz and I can handle clean up."

She rolls her pretty green eyes and continues. "I need to run home and shower and get changed. I can meet y'all after?"

"Sounds good." We agree to meet at a big box furniture store in two hours to start our day of shopping.

CHAPTER 18
ASHLEY

'd like to say I slept well last night and that thoughts of a certain cocky, blond lawyer didn't keep me awake.

But I'd be lying.

I tossed and turned all night long on his plush Italian leather sofa, my brain and my body battling it out while my heart sat on the sideline, sulking over his umpteenth rejection.

On one hand, I'm hard up, and from our small make-out session, my body is begging for release.

On the other, my brain is outraged, stomping and shouting, wondering why my stupid heart and body continuously allow him to best us again and again, all the while coming back and begging for more, like an orphan with a tin cup. *"Please Mr. Banks, can you reject me some more?"*

Luckily, my shower head helped with the release issue—well, it took the edge off, at least. I have a feeling the only thing that'll fully satiate my need for him is... well...*him.*

In desperate need of clarity, I FaceTime Mallory. After a few rings, her smiling, radiant face fills my screen. "Ash! How are you?"

"Eh. Kind of in the middle?" I shrug. "How are thou, fair maiden?"

She rolls her eyes. "Little weirdo. I'm great. Why are you in the middle?"

I inhale deeply, breathing out Colton's name with my exhale.

"Did your meeting with hot lawyer not go well?"

"It went okay."

"Ashley. Either spill the beans or—"

"Okay, okay! I met his son yesterday." I quickly fill my bestie in on everything that's transpired since we spoke yesterday.

"Well," Mally says before licking her lips and swallowing. "That's a lot to take in."

"Yup."

"What are you gonna do?"

I hesitate, knowing she is going to give me shit for my answer. "Anything I can. That little boy needs someone on his side—not that Colton isn't, because he *so* is. For someone usually cold, he looks at the kid with so much love in his eyes, I get secondhand feels from it. But Cruz is…there's a reason he won't talk to anyone, and the fact that he's gifted me with his voice…I will do anything to make sure he never feels abandoned again."

"I swear, you have more heart than common sense. You realize that by sticking around to help out, you're gonna end up falling for him and ending up with a broken heart, right?"

"About that…" I hedge, knowing she *really* won't like this.

"Ashley Louise Murphy."

"He-is-my-soulmate!" I rush the words out in seamless garble.

My bestie buries her face in her hands. "Oh, Ash."

Her sympathetic tone pickles. "Look, I know you think I'm a nut. But I feel it—all the way down to the marrow of my bones—he's my soulmate. We're meant to be together; it's just taking him a little more time to see it."

She offers me a sad smile. "Okay, Ash. If you say so."

"I do," I say, nodding vehemently. I stand firm in my beliefs, regardless of the opinions of others, even those of my best friend. She doesn't know what it was like when I first laid eyes on him. She didn't experience the full-body tingle, belly flutters, or racing heart I did. She didn't look at him and see home, but I did. One look at Colton Banks was all it took for me to fall, and I know sooner or later—though probably *much later*—he'll come around. And until then, I'm content to wait.

What I'm not going to do is be his doormat. His client, sure. His friend, you betcha. His go-between with Cruz, all day long. But a silly little girl with hearts in her eyes for him to string along—never again.

"Okay, then. Just…be careful."

I know she's coming from a good place—that she cares about me and seeing me hurt makes her hurt, so I paint on a smile I don't really feel and promise her I'll guard my heart while I wait before ending our chat and getting dressed.

I go for comfort—leggings and a concert tee—before rushing out the door to meet my boys.

An hour later, we've selected furniture for Cruz's room—a queen-sized distressed metal frame and some weathered wood nightstands with a matching bookcase and dresser. With the big stuff behind us, we're free to move onto bedding and décor. I'm hoping his choices will tell us a little more about him.

"Do you see anything you like?" I ask as Cruz and I peruse the aisles, walking hand-in-hand while Colton trails dutifully behind us on buggy duty.

"I like the water ones."

"These?" I show him a sheet set covered in whales and sharks and palm trees.

He nods eagerly, reaching out toward the sheets with grabby hands.

"Perfect." I quickly hunt down the matching quilt as well as a few toss pillows and curtains, adding them all to the cart. "Do you like the beach?"

Cruz's eyes drop to his scuffed-up tennis shoes. "I don't know. I-I might?"

"Have you ever been?" Colton asks.

He shakes his head.

"You wanna?" I ask, mentally checking items off our list.

"Yeah." A few minutes later, I feel a tug on the hem of my shirt. "Can I get this?" Cruz whispers, clutching a stuffed octopus to his chest.

Not wanting to overstep, I look to Colton. "Of course, bud. You can get anything you want. Today is all about you."

His blue eyes light with wonder. "Anything?" he asks, aloud, shocking us both. That one word—it's the very first he's spoken directly to Colton, and judging by the glassy look in his eyes and tremble of his chin, it didn't go unnoticed by him.

"Anything."

Even after being given the green light to go buck wild, Cruz only picks out a few nautical-themed knick-knacks to decorate his new room. His reluctance breaks my heart a little, because most kids would go hog-wild.

Once we hunt down a table lamp, an area rug, and a plush navy-blue chair, we head to check out and then to lunch.

Several hot dogs and milkshakes later, we're hitting up my favorite place on earth—Target.

"Do you want to take Cruz to look in the Dollar Spot, and I'll grab us some coffees?" Colton asks as we enter the hallowed doors.

"You mean Bullseye's Playground?" Poor clueless Colton, he doesn't know it, but he just pressed one of my hot buttons.

He cocks his head to the side. "Does it matter?"

"Uh, yeah, Colton. It does. The name Dollar Spot implies the items within it cost a dollar. Which is inaccurate. Some items are as high as ten dollars. I figured, as a lawyer, you'd at least appreciate transparency."

"Okay, then, would you like to take Cruz to *Bullseye's Playground?*" He emphasizes the words, making it clear he is only using the term to placate me—the asshole.

"Great. You can grab me a violet drink and"—I turn to Cruz—"do you want anything?"

He crinkles his nose. "No coffee."

"They have more than coffee, silly boy. Do you trust me to pick something for you?" I know asking him to trust me is a lot, but I'm hopeful all the same.

After a pregnant pause, he nods.

"Cruz will take a white chocolate crème Frappuccino."

Colton nods, sauntering over to Starbucks while Cruz and I peruse all of the little random happies lining the shelves before us. I squeal excitedly when I see two crab-shaped baskets.

Taking Cruz's grin as his seal of approval, I toss the baskets into our buggy. I also manage to snag a few random things for myself before Colton returns with our beverages.

Colton and I watch as Cruz tastes his drink. "Milkshake," he murmurs to himself before greedily slurping more down.

We start our Target run—officially—in the book section, loading the buggy with a variety of different age-appropriate books, before hitting up the toy section. Then Colton sends Cruz and me to look at clothes while he hits up electronics.

Three hours and an ungodly sum of money later, Cruz has damn near everything a kid could ask for. You know, aside from a loving, dependable mother—unfortunately, those can't be bought in stores.

CHAPTER 19
COLTON

loud nine. I'm on cloud nine, all because my son spoke to me. Sure, it was only one word, but it felt like someone hand-delivered me a check for a billion dollars.

Who knew all it took to feel like the king of the fucking world was one word?

After Target, I convince Ashley to join us for dinner at my place. Do-gooder that she is, she also helps lug up bag after bag. The furniture we bought was delivered before we got home and waiting in the lobby. By the time we get it all up, my living room looks like the stock room of a big box store.

"Are we doing takeout?" Ashley asks, claiming the sliver of cushion available next to Cruz, who is conked out on the couch.

"I planned on cooking."

She looks at me in disbelief. "You cook?"

"I'm not a chef by any means, but I can make a few dishes."

"It's a little early to eat though," she says, looking at the time on her phone.

"You wouldn't happen to want to build some furniture, would you?"

"Your fancy-ass building doesn't have a concierge or something that'll build it?"

I snort. "They totally do. But I want to build this for him. Plus, we only have to build the bed—thanks to them selling us the floor models."

"What about the old furniture?"

"That I had the concierge take care of."

She laughs, and I shrug.

"Then let's get to work, Mr. Banks. Show me what those hands of yours can do."

We both freeze at her words.

"Not like that—I mean show me how you handle your tools."

She slaps her hand over her mouth. I laugh.

"Oh my glob! No! That's also not what I meant."

"Pray tell, what did you mean, Miss Murphy?" I know damn well what she meant, but the pink hue of her cheeks is so lovely, I can't help but to tease her a little, all the while wondering how far down that blush of hers goes.

"I meant," she starts, speaking slowly and with intention, "let's work together to assemble the bed frame you purchased for your son."

"Oh, that makes more sense. Because I definitely thought you were coming onto me." I wag my brows suggestively, hoping like hell my out-of-character goofiness makes her laugh.

She stares at me for a split-second before the sweetest

sounding giggle bursts forth from those plump, highly kissable lips of hers. "Shut up and grab the box."

I raise two fingers to my forehead in salute before doing as she says. The guest room—Cruz's room—looks totally different without furniture. The only thing remaining is the mattress and box spring from the old bed.

The pale blueish-gray walls match the bedding he selected, which is convenient. Though, if he wants to paint the walls, I won't deny him. Hell, the kid has me so wrapped around his finger, I'd probably get him a pony if he indicated he wanted one.

After the bed frame is assembled, I drag the rest of the furniture into the room. At Ashley's recommendation, I position it against the wall. She says having one side closed off will help him feel more secure—I say anything is worth trying to make my son feel safe and loved.

I let Ashley dictate the rest of the furniture placement as well; she seems to have an eye for it, which is great seeing as I hired a designer to arrange the rest of my condo.

"Wanna help me bring the other bags back?" I ask, after breaking down the box from the bed frame.

"Yup." She hops up from her place on the floor. It takes us two trips to bring all of the bags back.

"You wanna break for dinner?"

"You cook, I'll decorate—that is, if you're cool with it."

If only she knew. "Knock yourself out."

She grins, rubbing her hands together. "Great! Holler when dinner's ready."

Tipping my imaginary hat to her, I happily leave my little purple-haired temptress to her own devices.

I wasn't kidding when I said I am only familiar with a few dishes. But the ones I know, I know well. A quick scan of my fridge and I know what I'm making: beef and broccoli lo mein. Both of my mothers love Chinese food, but as a kid we rarely had the money to buy the ingredients, much less eat out.

So, Mama K would whip up some with the things we could get our hands on—twenty-five cent Top Ramen, produce from the bargain bin, eggs, and soy sauce packets they would bring home from work.

From taste, you'd never know Mama K spent less than seven bucks to make it, because it was full of love. Sounds cheesy, but it's true.

Now, I'm lucky enough to use top of the line ingredients, but one thing I haven't changed in her recipe is the use of the cheap ramen noodles. There's something about them that just reminds me of...*home.* Which is the exact feeling I'm hoping to deliver to my sleeping son when he wakes.

Thirty minutes later, I kill the burner and venture back to Cruz's room to check on Ashley. "The food's read—wow!" The amount of work she's done in half an hour is mind-boggling. His bookcase is full of books. The rug is centered in the room, and the curtains are hung. His new toys are organized and his bed made. She's somehow managed to take this from a designer guest room to a kid-friendly palace.

"You think he'll like it?" she asks, looking around at her hard work.

"Ash, this is...every little boy's dream come true. I almost want to show it to him before we eat just to see his face."

Her green eyes twinkle. "You called me Ash."

"Your point?"

She does a little shimmy-shrug. "You usually call me Ashley or Miss Murphy. You've never called me a nickname!"

"I'd hardly call Ash a nick—"

"Nope! It is! Just admit it, I'm adorable and you like me and we're totally BFFs."

"Sure, you're a client and a friend." I school my features, not wanting to give away my true feelings—that she's the kind of friend I wouldn't mind seeing sweaty and naked beneath me while she claws at my sheets and pants my name.

Ashley's smile drops, right along with my stomach. "Right. Let's, uh, let's go eat."

I'm not sure how I keep messing up the dynamic with her, but I do. Determined to do better, I trudge behind her into the living room, letting her take point on waking Cruz.

"Hey, bud," she coos as she kneels down beside the couch. "You wanna wake up and eat?"

He wipes his eyes and blinks a few times before nodding.

"Awesome! Your dad cooked; doesn't it smell yummy?" Cruz sniffs the air like a puppy, and Ashley ruffles his already messy hair. "C'mon, let's eat. Then your dad has a surprise for you."

The word *surprise* sets him in motion; he jumps and races to the table, making both Ashley and me laugh. "You take a seat, too; I'll plate everything up and bring it out."

"Are you sure?"

"Positive. Go sit."

I dish up three bowls of lo mein and carry them out to the table before returning to pour three drinks—wine for the grownups and milk for Cruz. "All right," I say as I sit, "dig in!"

Cruz eyes the contents of the bowl skeptically, scrunching up his nose as he pokes at the noodles with his fork.

"It's delicious," Ashley assures him. "Try a bite."

He reaches into his bowl and plucks out a single noodle. I have to fight back a smile as he holds it away from his face, like it's a wriggling worm. After much hesitation, he pokes out his tongue and licks the noodle.

After another two licks, he nods and sucks the entire noodle into his mouth with a loud slurp. "That's good."

"You want to try the beef next?" She spears a piece on her fork and makes a big show of eating and marveling at how tasty it is. I know most of it's for show, but I still find myself wanting to beat on my chest in a show of masculine pride.

Cruz forgoes his fork in favor of his fingers again. He pinches the beef between his thumb and index finger, bringing it to his nose to sniff. After deeming the aroma passable, he nibbles off a small bite. His blue eyes brighten as the flavors meet his taste buds. "Yum!" he whispers before popping the rest into his mouth.

Two-for-two, I'm feeling pretty damn unstoppable right now. That is, until Ashley tries cajoling him into trying the broccoli.

He shakes his head back and forth in staunch refusal.

"Why not?" Ashley asks. "It is super yum."

Again, he shakes his head. "Green things are yuck."

"Have you ever tried broccoli?"

Ashley's patience with him is a beautiful thing. She's like the kid-whisperer.

"No." He pushes his bowl away, a stubborn look settling on his face. "Mom never made me."

Bitterness overtakes me. *Fucking Kelsey.*

"Let's make a deal," Ashley says after a moment, "why don't you taste a tiny bite? You won't know if you like it unless you try it. If you like it, cool beans, and if not, you don't have to eat it. Okay?"

He thinks over her proposition before countering with one of his own. "If I taste it, can I have a cupcake?" My boy's a little lawyer in the making.

Ashley looks to me, and I nod. "Sure thing, bud. Give it a taste and you can have a cupcake for dessert—I have one more condition, though."

His shoulders slump, but I press on, because I know he'll like my offer.

"If you don't like the broccoli, you can pick it out, but you have to eat the noodles and beef no matter what. Does that sound fair?"

"Yeah," he says softly, speaking to me directly for the second time. I replay the single word again and again in my mind, treasuring the way his voice sounds directed at me.

He stabs a piece of the offending vegetable with his fork. This time it gets the sniff and lick test before he takes a minuscule bite. He chews and chews before going back for a second taste.

Ashley and I wait with bated breath as he makes his

deliberation. Finally, he nods, giving it his seal of approval before devouring the rest.

Once we've sufficiently gorged ourselves on lo mein and dirt cupcakes, Ashley and Cruz clear the table and load the dishwasher, claiming it's their turn since I cleaned up last night. The whole ordeal is incredibly domestic—like we're one big, happy family.

The craziest part…I really fucking like how it feels.

CHAPTER 20
CRUZ

think I like it here. Everything is bright and shiny and new.

The man…Colton…my dad, like most of Mom's boyfriends, is so tall. But he's different than her boyfriends, too; he's nice and he never yells at me or hits me.

And he took me to the store today and said I could get anything I wanted. *Anything!* I thought he was lying. Mom used to pinch me whenever I asked for stuff. Sometimes it left bruises. Other times, her pointy nails would make me bleed.

She pinched me anytime I said anything, really—so, I just stopped talking. I thought she would like me more if I was quiet, since my voice made her so mad. It didn't work though.

She used to say it wasn't me she was mad at—just our circumstances. But I don't know what that means.

What I do know is the pretty purple lady is soft. She's soft and smells nice and has short nails and never rushes me or yells. I like her. She makes me feel…normal.

I'm not, though. Mom's last boyfriend called me a freak. I heard him say it once. I was supposed to stay in the laundry room, but I sneaked out because I needed to potty, and I heard him tell my mom he wanted to be with her, not play stepdaddy to a little freak. That was a few days before she left me here.

Colt—my dad—wasn't lying, though. He even let me get Ollie—my new red octopus. He's so squishy and cuddly, I want to keep him forever.

Daddy gives me a lot of food, too, even if some of it is weird looking. The green trees—*broccoli?*— wasn't my favorite, but they really wanted me to taste it, and I didn't want to make them angry after all of the nice things they did for me. And I got a cupcake. I think I'd do anything for a cupcake.

"Do you want to go see your new bedroom?"

I swallow the lump in my throat. *New bedroom*— which means the one I slept in last night with the big window isn't mine. The idea of a new room makes me sad, but I won't cry. Grownups hate it when kids cry. I look over to the big man who looks just like me and nod.

No matter what, it'll be better than my room at Mom's house. There, I slept on the sour-smelling couch with a towel for a blanket and no pillow.

I look to Ashley, and she nods. So, I do, too.

I'm confused when we go to the room I slept in last night. *How can my old room be my new one, too?*

Daddy opens the door, and Ashley guides me inside. All of the stuff we bought is in here! I don't know what to look at first, so I look at it all. The bed we picked out is in the corner with the soft, pretty blankets and sheets

—and Ollie, too! My bookcase is full of books and my new toys are here, too.

He meant it when he said this stuff was mine! *He meant it!*

I try my best not to cry, but I can't stop myself. I've never seen a room like this, except for on the TV, and now I have my own!

"You okay, Cruz?" my purple lady asks.

I wipe my tears, trying to hide them so she doesn't get mad.

She squats down next to me. "Are you crying because you're sad or because you're happy?" Her voice is like a hug instead of a punch.

She's not mad.

"Happy," I say. My voice sounds kind of like a frog, but they don't laugh at how funny it sounds.

Daddy drops to his knees, too. "This is your room, bud. These are your things, your toys. This is your special place. But I have something else for you, too."

He pulls a small box from his pocket and hands it to me. The wrapping paper is thick but I tear it away. I've never gotten a shiny, wrapped-up present before, and I want to see what's inside more than I want my next breath.

Under all the paper is a box. I shake it and something rattles around inside of it. I look to my purple lady, unsure, and she nods. I pop it open, and inside is a watch.

"This is a special spy watch," my dad says as he takes it from the box. "If you ever get lost, there's a special button you can push, and it will tell me how to find you."

A spy watch! That's awesome! I stick my hand out for him to help me put it on.

"Do you like it?" Daddy's voice sounds…nervous. Like he thinks I might not. But I really, really do.

"Does it make me a secret agent?"

The two grownups give each other a funny look.

"I saw a show about it once. The spy drove a fancy car like yours."

They look at each other again, and I worry they don't like me talking either. I zip my lips and drop my eyes to my shoes. I don't want Dad to take me back to my mom's.

"You mean James Bond?" he asks.

I nod.

"Yeah, except you're Agent 005."

"Because I'm five?" I slap my hand over my mouth—*I didn't mean to talk!*

"That's right, bud. And I can be…Agent C. What do you think?"

Another nod.

"Can you tell me with your words?"

I turn my head. *Does he for really real want me to talk?* "Yeah. C-can she be Agent Purple?"

My purple lady laughs her pretty laugh; it sounds like flowers and bumblebees and makes my tummy feel like Jell-O. "I'd be honored, dude!"

"C-could we watch it? Before bed?" I ask, feeling braver now that I'm a secret agent.

"I don't think James Bond is age-appropriate," Dad says with a doubtful look.

I frown.

"Oh! I know! Come on," Ashley says, leading us out to the couch.

She turns on a show with a girl agent who goes on missions with her friend who is a boy. My purple lady says it's called "Kim Possible." I love it—especially Rufus the naked mole rat.

My eyes keep closing, but I don't want to sleep. Today was the best day ever, and I don't want it to end. My dad puts his arm around me and snuggles me close. His big arms make me feel safe…*he makes me feel safe.*

I try my hardest to stay awake, but I can't keep my eyes open. The last thing I remember before falling asleep is hearing my daddy whisper that he loves me and is so glad I'm here.

CHAPTER 21

COLTON

n between emails, I scroll through the pictures Ashley sent me over the weekend. Even with a cell phone, she's a photography whiz. Looking at these images, you'd never know Cruz and I had just met; she somehow managed to capture us perfectly.

The amount of love I have for my boy is almost shocking. In such a short amount of time, he's become my everything, which is why today better be the big day.

Bright and early on Monday morning, Cruz and I submitted our DNA at the lab to confirm paternity. That's right—confirm, not test, because he is absolutely mine.

They said the results would take two to three days. And it's been five. Five days. To say I'm crawling out of my skin would be putting it lightly. I desperately want—no, need—to hear the words. To know heart, mind, body, and soul that he's mine.

If I don't get the results today, that means waiting through the weekend. Which is fucking unacceptable. I want to be able to sit my son down and tell him he is irrevocably mine. I want to see my name on his birth certificate. Cruz sharing my last name—which thankfully, Kelsey had the good sense to give him—isn't enough.

And the only thing standing between me and my goal is the results of this damn test.

As they've done all day, my eyes ping between my work and the clock. According to the lab's webpage, they're only open for another hour. *Someone better call me within the next forty-five, or so help me God, I'm calling them.*

I make it half an hour before I find myself dialing the lab. After two transfers and a lengthy hold, I have the results.

"Again, my apologies for the delay."

"These things happen," I say, my voice stiff.

"That they do, but your patience is appreciated all the same."

As soon as I end the call I jump up from my desk and head for the door. I'm nowhere near done with my tasks for the day, but they can wait for tomorrow, because right now, I need to pick up my son so we can celebrate.

I fly to Ashley's place and pound on the door. "Colton! Hey. You're really early. Is everything okay?"

Gratitude and euphoria and longing hit me like a ton of bricks all at once. Before I can think better of it, I have Ashley in my arms, holding her to me in a tight embrace.

"Everything's perfect." I speak the words against the smooth skin of her neck, breathing in her sugary scent.

"Okay," she says slowly, wriggling in my hold. "Not that I don't love hugs, but you're kind of freaking me out."

I release her, smirking all the while. "We're going out to celebrate."

"To celebrate—oh my glob! You got the paternity results!"

"I did." Now she's the aggressor, launching herself right back into my arms.

"Let me get Cruz and y'all can be on your way."

She turns to call after my son, but on impulse, I stop her. "I said *we,* that means you, too. Get changed."

"Me? Are you sure?"

Honest to God, I'm not sure, not at all. But something—some deep, hidden part of me saw her—and demanded I ask her to join us. And so, I did; I only wish I understood why.

Nevertheless, I lie and say, "One hundred percent. Wear something fancy."

"Yes, sir," she murmurs before skipping off, leaving me to find Cruz. I take a minute to collect myself—to will away the semi she brought on by calling me sir in that honeyed voice of hers.

A few deep breaths and several decidedly *unsexy* thoughts later, I wander further into the house in search of my son. I find him seated at the dining room table with a phonics book spread open before him.

In the short week Ashley has been keeping him for me, she has gone above and beyond to not only babysit, but to teach him, to nurture him, to love him. She's a purple-haired, crazy-making godsend.

He looks up when he hears me approach. His confusion at seeing me before his usual pick-up time quickly gives way to excitement in the form of a cheek-splitting smile.

"Hey, 005." I take a seat beside him. "Did you and Ashley have a good day?"

"Yeah. We played Candy Land and Gold Fish and had macaroni with hot dogs for lunch—it's my new favorite."

A triumphant grin tugs at my lips at his lengthy reply. In all, Cruz is still a quiet kid. Unless it's Ashley, he tends to keep to himself, but he's giving me more and more of his words when I speak to him.

"Go Fish is a fun game," I say, correcting him gently, "but I really like War. I'll teach you one day if you want?"

He nods. "Yes. Please."

"It's a done deal. Are you hungry? I took off work early to take you and Ashley to dinner."

His stomach growls, answering for him.

"Someone has a rumbly tummy," Ashley says, waltzing into the room, looking like pure temptation wrapped in a form-fitting dress that calls attention to every asset she has.

The golden-yellow hue makes her lavender hair pop and her skin glow, while the sweetheart neckline all but shines a spotlight on her tits. The stretchy fabric skims her sides and hugs her ass much in the same way I'd like, too. *Holy shit, I'm jealous of a dress.*

"I am," Cruz tells her, looking as smitten as I feel. "You look really pretty."

"Why, thank you. You're handsome yourself, bud."

I preen internally, because hello, the kid looks just like me.

"Are y'all ready?" She looks from Cruz to me.

"Very much so." I stand and find that in her heels she's actually the same height as me. With any other woman, that would be a turn-off, but with her, it's plain hot.

After helping Ashley into her seat, I buckle Cruz into his booster. The entire drive, my eyes keep sliding her way, as if drawn by a magnet.

"Where are we going?"

"I made reservations at Anson's." I drop my right hand to the center console, my fingers brushing the side of her arm in the small space.

She shivers at the contact but plays it off. "Oh, yum. I've shot a few rehearsal dinners there!"

"Best steaks in the city. Oysters, too." Ashley makes a face, and I laugh.

At the restaurant, the hostess promptly guides us to our table, leaving us with our menus and the promise of our server being by soon.

We chat idly between ordering drinks and dinner. I go for the oyster and filet surf and turf with hollandaise, whereas Ashley goes for the shrimp pasta. Cruz, my brave little guy, selects the kid's beef tenderloin with garlic mashed potatoes and broccoli.

We each taste small bites of one another's food. Ashley's pasta gets added to my go-to list; Cruz vows to never eat another oyster for as long as he lives.

Once our bellies are full and the plates cleared, I decide it's time to share the lab results with Cruz.

"You remember earlier this week when we went and had our cheeks swabbed?"

"The mouth Q-tip?" He shudders and sucks down some of his Shirley Temple.

"Yeah, that." God, this kid is cute. "Long story short, it was a special test to prove that I'm your daddy."

He gives me a funny look but doesn't say anything.

Ashley speaks up, throwing me a bone. "What your daddy is trying to say is the test says he is one hundred percent your daddy, and now no one will ever be able to say you don't belong with him, because you very much do."

Cruz smiles. "Good. That's good."

"Are you happy?" I ask him.

"I am," he whispers before grinning deviously. "But cake would make me even more happier."

The rest of the evening is spent in celebration with a slice of triple layer chocolate cake the size of Cruz's head, unending laughter, and a whole lot of love.

CHAPTER 22
ASHLEY

"Okay, dude, it's time for lunch!" I announce, setting Cruz's plate on the small table in my dining room.

He comes running in, tripping over his feet in his haste, like a basset hound puppy with too-long ears.

"You hungry?"

"Yeah." He parks himself in what he's dubbed as *his* chair and tucks into his PB-P-and-J sandwich. I watch as he takes a bite, waiting for him to get to the crunch. "This is different," he says once he swallows.

"Different good or different bad?"

He thinks for a minute before taking another bite. "Good. It's crunchy. I like it."

"I put some pretzel rods on it. It's how I like mine, too." I wink, causing him to grin.

"It's my new favorite."

His declaration puts a cheek-splitting smile on my face. I've been keeping him for two weeks now for Colton during the weekdays while he works—unless I have a shoot, then Stacia watches him. We try something new each day, and every time, it's his favorite.

Which is fitting, because this kid—*he's* my favorite.

He's been talking to me more and more every day. While he now answers all of my questions, he's never initiated a conversation. He talks to Colton more, too, but still reverts to nods and head shakes when he's nervous or can't fully read the situation.

Imagining what he might have gone through to make him mute nearly breaks my heart. The only thing keeping it from cracking completely is how freaking strong he is.

"What do you want to do after we eat?" I ask him, biting into my own PB-P-and-J.

"Can we…draw?" This is the second time he's asked to do some kind of art project this week—and it's only Tuesday. I make a mental note to hit up the arts and crafts store as soon as possible.

"We absolutely can. You got anything in mind?"

"It's a surprise."

"Oooh." I rub my hands together. "I love surprises!"

"Will you draw with me?"

"I will."

Cruz beams like he's just been given a lifetime supply of ice cream. And me…knowing I'm the reason for that smile of his, I feel like the coolest babysitter on the entire planet. Hell, maybe in the whole galaxy.

After lunch, we spend the next hour coloring. Cruz had me set up a divider to keep our papers private. I'm tempted to peek at his, but I worry it would break his fragile trust in me, so I keep my eyes on my own page.

"Okay, I'm done," he announces, scooting his chair back from the table. "Are you?"

"Almost," I tell him, putting the finishing touches on my picture. "There! Wanna trade on the count of three?"

"Yeah."

We count together and swap pages. Tears instantly well in mine when I see his. It's composed of three stick figures. The one on the left is wearing a tie, the one on right has a triangle-shaped body and a shock of purple hair, and the one in the middle is half the height of the figures on either side of him.

"It's a…family picture," he murmurs so softly I almost miss it. "'Cause you and Daddy are my family, right?"

"Yes, sweet boy. We're your family. Always."

"D-do you like it?"

"I love it!"

"Do you think Daddy will, too?"

"Bud, I bet he'll even hang it on the fridge!"

Cruz's blue eyes glow like twin lanterns. "Really? On the fridge? His big, shiny one?"

"I bet so. Better yet, I know so." Because I'm going to text his ass as soon as Cruz lays down to rest and make sure he knows how much this means to his son. Not that I think he'd balk at it—*he just might not be so happy to have me in their family portrait.*

We clean up and then I situate Cruz on the couch to rest. I don't make him nap, per se, but he does have to chill out and have quiet time for thirty minutes to keep him from getting overstimulated, per Stacia's suggestion.

Like I've done every day for the past two weeks, as soon as he's settled, I step into my office and scour the internet for any traces of Megan Grace and her bitch brigade. She's been suspiciously quiet for the last week or so. Part of me thinks she took the cease and desist seriously; another part of me thinks it's foolish to think I could get rid of her so easily. I guess only time will tell.

I check a few more sites before pulling out my phone to text Colton.

ME

FYI, Cruz drew you a picture. I promised him you'd hang it on the fridge.

COLTON

adds magnets to shopping list Sounds good. How is he?

ME

He's amazing. Resting right now while I do a little work.

COLTON

Still all quiet on the Megan front?

ME

So far so good. You think she's done tormenting me?

COLTON

Too soon to say for sure, but outlook is good.

ME

Okay, who are you and where's my Colton?

COLTON

Your Colton, huh? That's presumptuous.

ME

SEE! That's what I mean. In less than
two minutes, you've cracked a joke and
quoted a Magic 8 Ball. And not to
mention, the real Colton would have
100% said something cutting about not
being my anything. So, again, I ask
WHERE IS THE REAL COLTON?

COLTON

stands up I'm right here.

ME

OMG! And now an Eminem reference.
I'm calling you an ambulance; clearly,
you're ill.

COLTON

Not ill, Ash. Just in a good mood.

ME

Okay, well, I'll see you in a few hours.

COLTON

If you happen to cook dinner before I
got there, I wouldn't hate it…

ME

Did you seriously just ask me to make
you a sandwich?

COLTON

laughing emoji A grilled cheese does
sound delicious.

ME

You. Emoted. Nope. No. I'm calling
West, you've been body snatched.

I rock a perma-grin the rest of the day after our little texting session. Since I've been watching Cruz, we've definitely grown closer. Some days, he treats me like a client, others like a friend, but my favorite of all are the days where he looks at me like he wants to eat me whole when he thinks I'm not looking. Which makes this fun and flirty phone-banter a problem, because light and carefree Colton is honestly kind of sexy—and the last thing that man needs is more sexy.

I'm working on chopping tomatoes for my soup while Cruz washes the carrots. Me and my little sous chef work together like a well-oiled machine in the kitchen.

Cruz sniffs the air as the scent of the garlic and onion sautéing in the bottom of my pot fills the kitchen.

"Smells good, huh?" I ask, taking the freshly cleaned carrots from him to chop.

His little button nose crinkles up. "Are you sure I'm gonna like this?"

"I can't promise that you will, but you won't know if you don't try, right?"

My little warrior steels his spine and nods. "Right. What can I do now?"

"After I chop these bad boys up, you can help me stir them in."

"They look gross."

"Carrots give you superpowers."

"Do not."

"Okay, you're right. They don't—but!—they do contain beta-carotene."

"Beta-what-o-teen?"

"Beta-carotene. Your body uses it to make vitamin A and vitamin A helps your eyes."

"Hmmm." He eyes the orange sticks carefully.

"Hey, all I'm asking is that you try it. I won't make you eat something you don't like."

"Do secret agents like trying new things?"

I hand him the big wooden spoon and instruct him to stir slowly as I add the questionable veggies to the pot before answering his question. "Secret agents *love* trying new things. That's part of why they're so brave."

"I'm gonna be brave, Agent Purple."

"I know you are, Agent 005."

Thirty minutes later, dinner is ready, and our special dessert is in the oven. The only thing missing is Colton.

A knock sounds at the door. *There he is now.* I check the peephole, just in case, before letting him in.

He's smiling, so I assume his good mood is still in effect—lucky me. Or maybe I should say *unlucky,* because the man is attractive scowling, but smiling... he's downright lethal.

"Something smells good," he says, his voice a gruff growl. He inhales deeply as he shuffles past me, almost as if he was sniffing me, but that's preposterous. Right?

"Cruz and I made dinner."

"Right." He takes a step back from me. "What's on the menu?"

"You'll have to wait and see. Cruz is in the living room. Y'all can go to the table and I'll bring out dinner."

"Let me help."

"Are you sure? I've got—"

Colton raises his index finger to my lips and shushes me. "I insist."

"Oh-okay," I manage to stutter out, utterly shocked by the stark intimacy of his touch.

Sure, there have been small touches here and there—small, casual, and platonic.

Or so I tell myself, because allowing myself to momentarily imagine that the brush of his fingers across my lower back is anything more than friendly is detrimental to my mental—and sexual—health.

Don't forget his eyes, my brain unhelpfully adds, *the way he always knows where you are in a room…the way he looks at you when he thinks you're not paying attention…the way his eyes drop to your lips when you talk…*

I kindly tell my brain to shove it. A few accidental touches are nothing to shake a stick at. At least, that's what I'm choosing to believe it is, for now. I know we'll end up together—it just isn't our season yet.

He trails behind me to the kitchen. "Where do you want me?" he asks, leaning against the wall with his thumbs hooked into his belt loops.

Talk about a loaded question. I can think of multiple ways to answer it: in my bed, on your knees, in my heart. Instead, I settle for, "Can you grab three bowls from the cabinet to the right of the sink?"

"You got it." He strides across my small kitchen in two steps. I'm entranced as he reaches up to the second shelf. I can see his muscles bunch through the material of his button down. He has the kind of body that comes from a mixture of good genes and hard work; simply put, he's delectable, and I can hardly wait to get a real taste of him.

Colton places the bowls on the counter next to the plates I took down before he arrived. I ladle out three portions of soup before pulling my pan of grilled cheese sandwiches from the oven where they were warming and plate them up as well.

"Holy shit! You actually made—"

"Just wait until you taste it. I made us a grownup version and Cruz the classic American cheese version."

"Hell yeah." He comes up behind me at the counter, close enough that the heat of his body sears into mine. His nose skims my neck, and I have to clutch the lip of the counter to stay upright. "Everything in here looks delicious." His voice is back to that low growl from when he walked in; the sound of it does all kinds of things to me—like make my panties wet and my nipples hard.

"Let me give you a hand." He reaches around me and grabs a plate, spins away from me, and grabs another. "C'mon, little temptress, we want to eat it while it's hot, right?"

He winks and disappears into the dining room, leaving me panting and confused in his wake.

I crank the cold water at the sink and let it run over my wrists, splashing a little on my face to quell the raging hormone fire Colton ignited within me before carting our bowls of soup to the table.

My boys are already seated, patiently waiting.

I place the fullest bowl in front of Colton and the smallest in front of Cruz, saving the medium-filled bowl for myself—*glob, we sound like the three bears.*

"What makes my sandwich grown up?" Colton asks, poised and ready to take a bite.

"The fillings. Red pepper, garlic, sharp white cheddar, tomato slices, spinach, and bacon."

Colton eyes his grilled cheese with a new appreciation. "Hell. Yes," is all he says before digging in.

Cruz watches his dad for a few seconds before chomping into his sandwich the same way. They eat like barbarians, leaving breadcrumbs all over their plates and the table.

Since I'm not a heathen, I dip my sandwich into my soup, enjoying it in dainty—kidding, I devour mine, too.

"You gonna try your soup?" I ask Cruz, knowing he is apprehensive about all of the vegetables inside.

"It's really red."

"Yeah, it is. That's from the tomatoes."

"You like ketchup, right?" Colton asks.

Cruz nods. "A whole lot."

"Same thing. Think of this like warm ketchup soup."

The thought repulses me, but Cruz seems intrigued. We both watch as he swirls the red liquid with his spoon before dipping it in and scooping some up. He sucks the tiniest amount into his mouth before going back and eating with the same gusto he did his sandwich.

"Guess you like it?" his dad asks.

"It's my new favorite thing!"

My heart warms at his sweet praise. "You wanna show your dad the picture you drew?"

Without a word, Cruz pushes back his chair and darts off in search of his artwork. Not even a minute later, he flies back into the room with his paper clutched to his chest. He proudly hands it to Colton, waiting for his praise.

"Is that me?" he asks his son.

His blond head bobs as he nods.

"And is that you?"

Another nod.

"And that's…Ashley?" His voice sounds odd, kind

of foggy, as he asks his son about the purple-haired woman in the drawing.

"Yeah, Daddy. That's Agent Purple. She's our family, too, right?"

Tears fill my and Colton's eyes, though he hides his far better. Cruz has never called him daddy to his face.

A myriad of emotions plays across Colton's face like it's a movie screen. Sadness dances with delight as he wrangles back his tears. In the time it takes him to get them under control, Cruz's face drops.

"Bud," I say, but he's already gone, running toward the living room.

"Damn it!" Colton whisper-yells.

"Hey, you didn't do anything."

"He thinks I hate it."

"But you don't, and once you explain it to him, he will be okay."

"You think?"

"I know. You're such a good dad, and that little boy loves you." I stand from the table and extend a hand toward Colton. He stands as well. "C'mon, let's go find your son."

We find Cruz curled up in a ball in the corner of the room next to my television cabinet. His little shoulders shake with sobs, but he never makes a sound.

Colton and I both sit down on the floor, close enough for him to know we're there, but far enough away to not crowd him. "Hey, bud, can we talk?" Colton asks. "Please?"

Cruz discreetly wipes his eyes, but his still-damp cheeks and red nose give him away.

"Why'd you run away? Did you think I was mad at you?"

He sniffles and nods.

"I'm not. Not at all, not even a little."

Cruz looks from his dad to me. "Will you come out and talk to us, Agent 005?" I ask him, patting the floor in front of us.

"O-o-okay." He crawls forward and sits up. "I-I'm s-s-sorry."

"Cruz, bud, no. You didn't do anything wrong. You…you called me 'daddy' for the very first time, and I got a little choked up. I wasn't mad, I was—am—I'm so, so happy. And you're right, Ashley is our family, too."

"You're happy?" Cruz scoots forward a smidge. "With m-me, you're happy?"

Tears cloud my vision as Colton nods his head. "Happier than I've ever been. I love you, bud."

Cruz shocks us both when he launches himself into his father's arms, nearly tackling him to the floor with the force of his hug. "I love you, too, Daddy."

CHAPTER 23
COLTON

sit with my son on my lap, holding him tightly to me as I rock us back and forth, murmuring in his ear all the while about how much I love him and how much better my life is with him in it. I don't have a clue of how much time passes as I reassure my boy that he's safe and wanted and so fucking loved.

At some point, Ashley joins us, rubbing Cruz's back as his tears—happy ones now—ebb. On every down pass, her fingers brush mine, and with every brush, a sense of rightness fills me. Cruz was spot on when he said she was our family—the question now is—in what capacity?

The three of us stay on the floor until Cruz's tears give way to sleep. Poor dude tired himself out with all those big emotions.

"Do you want me to carry his stuff down or..." Ashley trails off.

"Or what?" The words come out as a challenge, but I'm genuinely curious as to what she may offer.

"Or you could stay?" She says the words slowly,

before rushing to add, "for dessert. Cruz and I made brownies!"

I lick my lips. "Mmm. You'll never hear me turn down brownies. Where do you want me to put him?"

"You can put him in my bed if you want? That way we can watch a movie or—was that presumptuous, for me to think you'd want to stay that long?"

I'd love to tell her nothing's presumptuous when it comes to her, but that would be inappropriate. Instead, I smirk and say, "A movie sounds fine."

"Second door on the right," she calls over her shoulder on her way to the kitchen.

I stand carefully, as to not wake Cruz, and head back to Ashley's bedroom. Stepping into her bedroom is over-whelming—it's like having Ashley on every side of me, the space is so intrinsically her.

From her scent hanging in the air to the deep teal accent wall, this space is all *Ashley*. Her bed, a massive golden, canopy-style bed—minus the actual canopy—sits centered on the accent wall. It's topped with the thickest comforter I've ever seen, cream in color and feather soft.

With one hand, I knock a few of the five-hundred decorative pillows to the floor before laying Cruz down onto the bed. He hums contentedly in his sleep, immedi-ately rolling to his side as his little body sinks down into the mattress. A charcoal throw blanket is artfully arranged at the foot of her bed; I use it cover Cruz, tucking him in before pressing a kiss to his forehead.

I know I should head back out to the living room, but the urge to explore has me rooted to the floor. My feet propel me toward the small coral-colored dresser in the corner.

"What am I doing?" I mutter to myself. Even as I question my own sanity, my hands tug on the pull of the top drawer, sliding it open, revealing to me a pile of tangled lace and silk. In all my life, I've never rifled through a woman's things, much less have I ever had the urge. But Ashley…in her room, with her mouthwatering scent surrounding me, I feel helpless to resist.

I know it's wrong and perverse, and yet the knowledge doesn't diminish my need…my want. I want to rub each piece between my fingers so I can remember how they feel; I want to catalog every item so I can imagine her taking it off for me when I'm in my bed alone. Some sick, hidden part of me wants to pocket a pair so I can fuck the soft silk as I pretend it's her.

Footsteps sound down the hall. *Shit!* I slide the drawer closed just in time for Ashley to step into the room. "Is everything okay—what are you doing?"

"Nothing," I say, sounding as shady as I look. She may as well have caught me red-handed. Even as a lawyer, I'm struggling to come up with other probable causes that land me facing her dresser in the corner of the room with a tent in the front of my slacks.

"Nothing, huh?" She tilts her head to the side and taps her index finger against her chin. "Turn around then."

"Sure thing. Just"—I reach down to adjust myself—"give me a minute." Certain she won't see the evidence of my arousal, I pivot around to face her.

Her green eyes rove over my body, pausing at my fly before sweeping down and back up to meet my gaze. "What were you doing?"

"Admiring the paint color."

"Of my lingerie chest?"

I very nearly choke on my tongue—or maybe it's my desire for her—when the word lingerie leaves her glossy lips. Thoughts of what might be in the other three drawers plague me. "The contents are irrelevant," I say. The words sound like bullshit even to my own ears.

My entire body locks up as she crosses the room to stand toe-to-toe with me. "Really? You don't care? You're not even the least bit curious?"

I force a scoff. "Hardly."

She leans in, bringing her sugary scent close enough to taste, and reaches past me with her right hand. "Then why are my panties sticking out?"

I whip around to check with my own two eyes, a denial on the tip of my tongue.

"Gotcha!" She sounds so proud of herself for catching me in my lie.

Infuriating little temptress—I ought to take her over my goddamn knee.

My face is screwed up in a scowl to hide the embarrassment surely staining my cheeks. But Ashley pays me no mind. Instead, she wraps the tail of my tie around her fist and tugs. "C'mon, perv, let's go eat some chocolate."

After eating the most decadent brownies of my life and checking in on Cruz, Ashley and I settle down on the couch to watch a movie. Her couch is more of a loveseat, with only two cushions. She's on my right and close enough that our shoulders brush. It's an intimate arrangement, yet it feels right. Even if it is a little awkward at first.

"I, uh, can take the chair, if you want?" she asks.

I stretch my arms above my head, arching my back to relieve my stiff muscles before laying my right arm along the back of the couch. "No. Stay."

She glances to where my fingertips are grazing her exposed shoulder and then stares straight ahead. "What are we watching then?"

"Anything's fine with me," I say, far more concerned with my proximity to a certain little temptress than what's playing on the television.

A few clicks of the remote later and the screen goes dark as "Ain't No Rest for the Wicked" by Cage the Elephant fills the room. Words begin filling the screen, telling us how the angel Lucifer was cast out of Heaven and condemned to rule Hell—that is, until he decided he was due for a vacation. *What the what?*

"What is this?"

"Lucifer," Ashley says, shifting toward me ever so slightly. "I've been wanting to watch it. Is that okay?"

"Perfectly." Except every time Lucifer mentions punishing people, I picture myself punishing Ashley. In my mind, I take her over my knee and spank her ass red before rubbing and kissing away the sting.

And when he soothes the officer, telling him how it's fun to get away with things, I'm struck with a dangerous thought, an illicit desire—I *could get away* with fucking Ashley. No one has to know.

The show, coupled with the sexpot of a woman next to me, has all of my deep, dark desire rising to the surface; rising right along with my cock, which lays against my leg like a steel pipe.

With every small shift and adjustment, her lean, toned, warm body brushes mine. I'm burning up with longing, to the point my shirt and tie feel stifling. I yank at the knot with shaking fingers, and pop the top two buttons.

"Are you okay?" Ashley asks.

"Fine," I say, while my terse tone tells her I'm anything but.

Concern clouds her features as she turns to face me. "You look a little flushed." She presses the back of her hand to my cheek and then my forehead. "Feverish, even."

Jesus Christ, I want this woman so bad I'm feverish and flushed. Too bad the only cure for what ails me is her sweet, tight pussy milking my dick for all it's worth.

"I'm a little hot, that's all."

Ashley studies my face, searching for the truth. She won't find a hint of deception there, my mask is well practiced. *If she were to look down at my lap though…*

"You've got an undershirt on. Just ditch the button down." She says it so nonchalantly, like me stripping out of my shirt while sitting next to her watching a show about sin is the most normal thing ever.

I wrestle with the ethics of it, rationalizing all the while. On one hand, I *am* wearing a shirt underneath— even if it is sleeveless. On the other, the thought of stripping off the overshirt in front of her feels wrong— gateway sexy, if you will.

Fuck it.

I loosen my tie a little more and slip it over my head, tossing it to the coffee table as I stand. Ashley's chest rises and falls with each labored breath, her eyes laser-focused on my fingers as they pop the buttons one at a time.

The shirt slides down my shoulders, and I drape it over the coffee table. Her hungry gaze burns over me as

I reclaim my seat next to her. Now, our bare shoulders touch, my heated skin sticking to hers.

How is it that I'm hotter now, with less clothing on? Oh, yeah…probably because I'm imagining the little temptress next to me with less clothes on, too.

We're both only pretending to pay attention to the show, stealing glances at one another while subtly shifting closer together. It's a well-practiced dance we're engaged in.

I lean back into the couch, draping my arm around her; she leans slightly into me. I spread my knees further apart; she tucks her legs up and to the right, bringing her closer still.

A shift of my hips and we now have three points of bodily contact—shoulders, hips, and legs.

Shoulders, hips, and legs. The three words run through my mind like a chant as a vision unfolds within my mind's eye.

Her legs spread on either side of mine as she rides me, her hips pressing into mine while she holds tightly to my shoulders for balance.

Fuck, fuck, fuck. This desperate need I feel for her is about to boil over.

In a boss move, she stretches out her left leg, propping it on my lap. Two things happen all at once. She brushes my straining erection with her ankle while my eyes zero in on the space between her now split legs.

Her shorts are loose and flowy, the fabric falling just right to reveal a peek of her white lacy panties. Saliva pools in my mouth as I imagine how she feels there, how she tastes. I bet she's as sweet as the sugar she smells like.

My eyes flit to hers, only to find her staring straight

at me. She knows where I was looking, and she's damn sure about to chew me out. I deserve it. Only, the words never come. Instead, she shifts her right leg from beneath her and props her foot on the coffee table, giving me an unfettered view.

I pinch my eyes shut and curl my fingers into fists. The need to touch, to taste, to ravage her, is overwhelming me.

She rubs her foot over my dick, and my eyes fly open. "Ashley," I growl. "This is a dangerous game you're playing."

"We—*we're* playing. I know you want me every bit as bad as I do you."

"I'm pretty sure the Rolling Stones nailed it when they said 'you can't always get what you want.' As I've said, you're my client. Any kind of relationship, physical or otherwise is inappropriate."

"But you do…want me?"

I groan as her foot strokes over my dick again. "Clearly."

"Then show me."

Frustration mingles with my lust. "Didn't you just hear me? Touching you is wrong."

She grins wickedly. "I'm not asking you to touch me —I'm asking you to touch you. I want you to slip your big, hard dick out of those pants and fuck your hand like it was me. I want you to *show* me how much you want me."

"It's still wrong," I say, but my words lack conviction.

"I'd be happy to help." I go to rebuke her yet again, but the sight of her hand pushing her shorts and panties

to the side has my words dying in my throat. "A little…
visual aid, if you will."

She runs her index finger through her slick folds,
gathering moisture before rubbing her clit. It's too much.
I'm helpless to stop myself. A man, a mere mortal, can
only take so much.

I free myself from the confines of my pants. I know
we agreed not to touch each other, but I can't stop myself
as I lean over and steal some of her cream for lubrication.

Her movements falter as my fingers skim over her,
but my hand is wrapped firmly around my aching dick
before she can fully react.

"Show me," she moans, "show me how you like to
be touched. Pretend it's me."

I squeeze my cock tighter and work my hand up and
down, giving a little twist every time I reach the head.
My free hand cups my balls, massaging and tugging.

She keeps working her clit with her right hand, while
her left explores. She dips her middle finger inside,
fucking herself with it, then she brings it to her lips,
smearing her juices over them before licking it off.

"Fuck, Ash." I grunt her name, thrusting up into my
hand with enough force to shake the couch.

"I'm so close, Colton." Her voice is wanton and
reedy, full of need.

She needs this release as badly as I do.

"Come for me, Ash. Come all over your fingers."

She doubles down her efforts, her hips chasing her
fingers as she rubs herself to completion. "Yes, Colt
—yesss!"

Rope after rope of hot release lands on my chest as
she climaxes with my name on her lips.

As the lustful fog of the moment clears, clarity comes rushing in, along with a heaping dose of shame.

Leaning forward, I snatch my shirt off the table and clean up the mess on my stomach. I ball up my now-soiled shirt and stand, tucking myself back into my slacks as I do.

It's like she emits pheromones designed exactly for me. She's a temptation like no other. And definitely a witch—one who has absolutely ensnared me with her spell.

"Ashley," I start, my voice firm but gentle, ready to let her down easy, but she cuts me off.

"No!" She stands as well, righting her shorts. "Nope. I'm gonna stop you right there. You are not about to tell me this was a mistake and that it can't happen again. You are not about to tell me how I'm not your type—you're about an orgasm too late for me to believe it. You are not about to tell me we can't be together, blah-blah-blah."

She's pacing now. No doubt, if this was a cartoon, her hair would be alive, swirling in the air with her anger.

"You don't get to dismiss me again. You don't get to take what happened here and sully it, because guess what, asshole?" She throws her arms wide to either side. "I'm not asking you for a commitment. I'm not begging you for a relationship. What we did was hot and raw and so-fucking-mutual. You don't want it to happen again? Fine, that is your prerogative. But you don't get to keep jerking me around simply because you can't make up your mind. Got it?"

I suck in a deep breath. "Got it."

"Great. Why don't you go clean up a little more and grab Cruz? I'll gather his stuff while you do."

Somehow, she's managed to flip the script. Now, I'm the one being dismissed, and honestly, I don't fucking like it—not one bit.

"Can do."

"Great," she says again. "I'll leave his bag by the door, please turn the bottom lock on your way out."

Guilt keeps me rooted in place. I want to apologize. To wax poetic over all the ways I do, in fact, want her. Instead, I say, "Am I still okay to drop Cruz off tomorrow morning?"

She laughs a hollow, dry laugh that sends chills down my spine. "Yup. You shouldn't punish a son for his father's transgressions." She turns and pads into the kitchen, giving me her back. "Bye, Colton."

With nothing else to do, I head down the hall to get Cruz, making a pitstop in the bathroom to wash my hands. He's still sleeping soundly—thank God—and doesn't even stir when I gather up his small body against my chest.

As promised, his bag is by the door and Ashley—she's nowhere in sight.

CHAPTER 24
ASHLEY

"Ugh," I groan into my hands before looking back up at my best friend's face filling my laptop screen. "Even Cruz can sense the tension between us."

Colton and I have spent the week tiptoeing around one another. Each morning, he's dropped off Cruz without a word to me, and each night, he's picked him with a simple "thank you" and a tip of his chin.

I haven't exactly made an effort to break the ice, but I also don't think I should have to. When it comes to him, it feels like I'm always the one bending and breaking.

I'm fed up with his hot and cold behavior. It's like the old saying, *one step forward, two back,* except we take about ten back. I'd think fate mismatched us, chalk it up to a little carnal lust, except for the way my heart goes haywire every time he comes around—every time I think of him, really.

"Kids are really perceptive," Mallory says. "Especially ones who are more used to observing. From what you've told me, Cruz is the kind of kid who drinks in his surroundings."

"I feel awful. He actually asked me yesterday if I wanted him to stop talking to me like his daddy did. Talk about having your heart stomped on."

"Oh, Ash." Mallory tears up. "Stupid pregnancy hormones, sorry! Give me a minute."

I wait while she wrangles her emotions.

"You two need to find a way to patch things up."

"I know. We do. I just feel like—"

"He needs to come to you, I get it."

"Yeah, but the man has more pride than sense, so, I'm not exactly holding out hope."

"Upside, it's Saturday, which means you get two days brooding lawyer free!"

"Woo-hoo." I spin my index finger through the air. "Enough about my stupid problems. Let's talk about those babies."

"Girl! I'm only sixteen weeks, and I feel like I'm stuffed full."

"I hear twins will do that to you."

"Ha-ha, funny girl."

"Thank you, thank you. I'll be here all night."

"You're such a delightful little weirdo."

I grin at my best friend right as my phone rings on the desk. I pick it up and glance down at the screen, my face screwing up in a frown when I see who's calling.

"Who is it?" Mally asks.

"Colton."

"Are you gonna answer?"

I sigh, because we both know I am.

"Hello, Colton."

He clears his throat. "Ash—ley. Hey. How are you?"

"I was enjoying my day off. I'm wedding free and just chilling."

Silence fills the line.

"Look, I'm not trying to be rude, but is there a reason you called?"

Mallory slaps a hand over her mouth as I rush to mute our video call.

"Yeah, sorry. I…I had something come up tonight, and I really need you to watch Cruz."

Now I'm the silent one.

"Can you be here around seven?"

"Are you for real right now? You spend the entire week ignoring me and now you want me to come watch your son so you can—what? Go out with West? Go on a" —I gulp— "*a date?*"

"Ashley." Somehow, he makes those two syllables drip with exasperation. *Well, right back atcha, Col-ton.* "Please? I…an opportunity of sorts fell into my lap, and I'd be a fool not to pursue it. However, without your cooperation, my hands are tied."

On my computer screen, Mallory is shaking her head. I'm not sure if she's trying to tell me no or is resigned to the fact that I'm about to say yes.

"Sure, Colton."

"You're the best!"

"For double our agreed-upon daily rate. Plus, money to order a pizza."

Colton laughs under his breath. "Sure thing. See you at—"

I cut him off. "I'm doing this for Cruz. Not for you. Just so you know."

His muffled laugh becomes a chuckle. "Loud and clear. See you at seven."

He ends the call and I toss my phone down to my desk. Mallory's lips are moving a mile a minute, but I can't hear a thing since she is still muted.

I wait for a lull in her tirade before turning her volume back on. "Are you even listening?"

"Nope. You were muted."

"Dammit, Ashley!"

"Listen, same song and dance—you were telling me I'm being dumb and to be careful. It's fine. I'm fine."

We chat a few more minutes before she has to go. I still have a few hours before I have to head to Colton's, and a nap sounds like the perfect way to pass the time.

I wake from my nap as refreshed as I am full of dread. In other words, I'm still exhausted. After a yawn and a stretch, I drag my feet to the kitchen to start a pot of coffee before hopping in the shower.

Thankfully, the combination of the steaming water and the piping coffee do the trick—I'm wide awake, if not a little grumpy.

I dress for comfort, knowing Cruz will want me to get down on the floor and play with him. Plus, it's not like I'm trying to impress anyone.

Not yet, anyway.

At seven on the dot, I knock on Colton's door. He swings it open with a smile on his stupid, handsome face. "Ashley, come in."

I flash him a contemptuous smile as I move past him and into the condo.

"Agent Purple!" A little blond ball rushes me, wrapping his arms around my waist. "I missed you!"

A genuine smile breaks forth. "You saw me yesterday, goofball."

He huffs. "That was forever ago. I wanna see you always. I don't like when you're not with us. On TV, families are always together."

Oh, boy. While I'm over the moon he's feeling so chatty, I'm ill-prepared for the topic.

I look to Colton for help, but he's busy on his phone. *Probably texting his date. Jackass.* I guess I'm on my own here. "There's all different kinds of families, bud. Sometimes you have a dad and a mom. Or sometimes, like your daddy, you get two moms or two dads. Some kids only have one parent. And others have step-parents."

"What's a step-parent?"

"It's when parents who aren't married to each other marry someone else."

His blue eyes twinkle. "That means…if you married my daddy…you'd be…my stepmom?" He bounces on his toes in excitement. I curl my toes in my shoes and clench my fists to keep from banging my head into the wall. This is going horribly wrong.

"Um, well." I cough a few times trying to get the big, blond jackass off of his phone. "Um, yes? Technically, whoever your daddy marries one day will, in fact, be your stepmom."

There. I pat myself on the back. *That was good.*

"Good. Then y'all can get mar—"

Nope. Not today, Satan. "Why don't we play a game?" I say, redirecting him.

"Can we play Chickapiglets?"

"Absolutely. Go run and grab it."

In his absence, I turn on Colton. "Are you kidding me? You just left me hanging there? I'm glad your phone is more important than your son."

I regret the words as soon as I say them. I'm being snotty, and while he deserves a bit of my anger, he doesn't deserve cruelty.

He glares at me but says nothing.

"Sorry," I mutter as Cruz bounds back into the foyer.

"Let's play!"

I shoot Colton one last apologetic look before giving Cruz all of my attention. "You got it, bud; let's play."

Fifteen minutes later, my little friend and I are deep into our game, working together to make matches, building our hybrids, and avoiding the poo. It's a weird little matching game, but I love the way it makes Cruz smile and that it encourages teamwork, which is perfect for him and Colton.

"I was thinking we'd get pizza?" I ask Cruz as our game comes to an end.

"Pizza sounds perfect," Colton says, making me jump.

"Why are you still here?" I ask. "Thought you had some mind-blowing, not to be missed opportunity tonight?"

His lips tip up. "I do."

"Okaaaay," I stretch the word. "Vague much?"

Instead of answering me, he turns to his son. "You ready?"

"Super ready!" he says, jumping to his feet.

"Ready for what?" I ask, getting to my feet as well.

"You'll see. Take a seat, we'll be back."

"Sure thing." I bite out the words, wondering why in the hell Colton asked me to babysit if he's going to be—

oh, I swear on I hold dear, if he brings his date here, I might actually murder him.

I play on my phone while I wait, scrolling through social media, checking for signs of life from Megan Grace. She's still strangely absent. Mallory and her girls, along with Stacia, all say it's a good thing. I think it's freaking suspicious. I know if I had some psycho personal vendetta to ruin someone, it'd take more than a strongly worded letter to get me to back down.

About twenty minutes pass before Cruz reappears. In the time he was gone, he's changed into a little suit, bowtie and all. He has his hair combed back away from his face, looking dapper and more like his father than ever.

"We're ready for you," he says.

"Ready for what?" I'm skeptical but I take his hand anyway.

He walks us back to the kitchen, where the picture I'm met with short circuits my brain.

Does not compute, is the only thing I can think. Because standing before me—also rocking a bowtie—is Colton. He's poised behind the island, which boasts a hefty floral arrangement comprised of stunning ivory roses intermingled with dahlias, irises, peonies, and delicately gorgeous anemones with lavender sprinkled throughout.

"That's gorgeous. Who's the lucky recipient?"

"I don't know what that word means, but they're for you," Cruz says proudly. "I helped Daddy pick it."

Like I'm the Grinch, my heart swells thrice its size in my chest—until weariness flies in and pops my happiness like a dart to a balloon. *Why did they get me flowers?*

"Consider them Act One of my apology."

"Act One?"

Colton nods. "Yes. It has three parts in total, with a brief intermission between the second and third."

"Oh, sure, okay." *Because that makes sense.*

"I hope you brought your appetite. I made Mama K's Shepherd's pie."

I'm on the verge of calling Colton on his shit, but Cruz's hope-filled smile has me biting my tongue. So, instead of demanding he tell me his motive, I say, "Food sounds great."

"005, will you seat our guest?"

"I will, Daddy."

Cruz offers me his arm again and walks me to the dining room. On the table is a miniature version of the bouquet in the kitchen. Cruz pulls my chair out for me and waits as I scoot myself in.

"What's going on, bud?" I ask, trying to get him to spill the beans.

"It's a surprise." The kid's lips are zipped; I guess I'll just have to wait and see.

Moments later, my boys—*no!*—Colton and Cruz return. Cruz is carrying a salad bowl while his dad handles the baking dish. They place them onto the table with flourish, and then Colton dishes out plates for each of us.

Colton gives me an inpatient frown when I don't immediately start eating. "What are you waiting for?" he asks, waving his fork around. "Dig in."

I place my napkin in my lap, and Cruz rushes to copy me. "What I'm waiting for is the other shoe to drop."

"Meaning…"

"Meaning what is this? You asked me to watch Cruz

so you could go out, so explain to me why we're all eating together?"

"Ash." He shakes his head. "For someone so incredibly smart, you're slow on the uptake, huh?"

"Oh, how nice. I have always enjoyed being insulted over dinner."

Colton rolls his striking blue eyes. "I'm just saying, it's fairly obvi—*ouch!*"

I don't bother hiding my smile as Cruz kicks his dad under the table.

"You're messing it all up, Daddy. Be nice!" He gives his father a meaningful look, one that borders on a glare and promises mutiny if he continues misbehaving.

"What I'm trying to say is that I'm sorry."

"Are you?" I raise my brows.

"Am I what?"

"Sorry. Are you sorry?"

Colton nods. "I am."

"Interesting." I bite into the Shepherd's pie. A symphony of flavors plays in harmony, serenading my taste buds. Creamy potatoes, kernels of corn, and tender, smoky barbecued pork come together to create a Shepherd's pie unlike any other I've had. "This is delicious."

"Interesting, how so? And thank you, Mama K taught me to make it; it was one of her favorites to cook when I was growing up. One of her jobs was at the pork plant over in Holly Bluff, and she'd bring some home every payday."

"Interesting because for someone who's trying to apologize, you haven't actually said the words, have you?" I take another bite. "Thank you for sharing this with me."

The fact that we're fighting while simultaneously

carrying on an unrelated conversation doesn't escape me. If anything, it speaks to the insanity that is Colton and me.

"She's a hell of a cook. Maybe you can try hers one day."

"What?"

"And I did apologize—what do you think all of this is?" He waves a hand in the air.

"I feel like we're going in circles. You have not actually said the words 'I'm sorry' except to say you were trying to say you were sorry."

"Daddy, just say it." Cruz has been watching the two of us like it's a ping-pong match.

"Fine." Colton clenches his jaw before saying those two coveted words. "I'm sorry."

I lean back in my chair, crossing my arms over my chest. "For?"

He frowns in consternation.

I smile. *Not so fun being left to try and explain adult things in kid appropriate terms, is it, jackass?*

"I'm sorry for..." He pauses. "The way I behaved Tuesday night. My inability to process my personal feelings isn't something I should take out on other people. I will do better from now on."

"Ah, the taste of crow," I murmur happily to myself before addressing Colton. "Forgiven. Now, tell me more about Mama K and..."

"Mama Mel."

"Have you told them about—" I nod my head toward the miniature version of the man across from me.

"I have. They are planning to visit soon to meet him. They wanted to give us time to get settled. They're excited to meet him—and you."

"Me?"

"Of course. I snapped a pic of Cruz's family portrait and sent it to them. They had about a million questions about you. So, I told them they could ask you all of them in person if they wanted answers."

"Lovely."

Colton nods, my sarcasm missing him entirely. "They are."

CHAPTER 25
COLTON

Now that Act One and our intermission—err, dinner—are both finished, it's time for Act Two. And by that, I mean dessert.

"Cruz, you wanna go grab the thing?"

"Yeah!" He shoots off like a rocket into the kitchen and returns with a small tin and places it on the table in front of Ashley.

"Thanks, bud," she says to him before looking to me. "What's this?"

"Open it!" Cruz and I say in unison, though his delivery is far more energetic.

"Okay, okay." Ashley holds her hands up in surrender before popping the lid on the tin. "What are these?"

"Cookies, Agent Purple. They're cookies." The *duh* is heavily implied in Cruz's tone.

"Half are peanut butter chocolate and the other half are peanut butter and fluff."

"Y'all made these?"

Cruz and I nod.

She takes a bite from each of the flavors, making a big show of how delicious they are. "Cruz! These are the best cookies I've ever had. My new favorite!"

My little guy jumps in the air. "That's what I said, too!"

I hold out my fist to him, and he bumps it. "Nailed it."

"I love that show!" Ashley says. "Thank glob you boys can bake better than those people."

"You maybe want to hang around and watch an episode or two?"

"Is that Act Three?" she asks.

"Pretty much. The plan was to blow you away with our culinary prowess and to convince you to stick around and spend time with us."

Cruz gives her his best puppy dog eyes. "Is it working?"

"Yeah, bud, it's working."

I send the two of them to the living room while I toss the dishes into the sink. When I head into the living room, I am shocked to find Ashley in the middle of the couch rather than Cruz.

"This way we both get to sit by Agent Purple," my son says knowingly. Little dude is working his Cupid angle hard. And while I like the way he's thinking, now's definitely not the right time.

Maybe one day, though. One day when she's not my client. When all of my focus doesn't need to be on making sure Cruz is coping and adjusting well. One day when I can sort my feelings and handle my shit like a grown-ass man and not belittle her for my own lack of control. *Yeah, maybe one day.*

"Works for me." I grab the remote and hit play before

settling down next to my little temptress. The ends of her purple hair brush my arm, and her sweet scent tickles my nose. Sitting by her is pure, delicious torture —and yet, I love it.

One episode of bad baking turns to the entirety of season one, and before I know it, it's well after ten and I'm begging her, once again, to stay the night.

"It's too late to drive."

"Colton—"

"We could take Cruz to the kids' museum tomorrow. And for brunch at Benny's."

"We can do that regardless of where I sleep."

"But—"

"I don't have a change of clothes, so I'll have to go home tomorrow anyway."

"Please," I beg, giving her my own version of Cruz's puppy eyes. I'm honestly not sure why I'm pushing this so hard. All I know is the thought of her leaving sends a hollow feeling through me.

My heart pounds in my chest, beating out a pleading rhythm while she deliberates. I feel like I'm asking her to go to prom rather than to sleep on my couch.

"No can do. But I'll happily meet y'all for brunch."

I'm tempted to keep pushing her, to get on my knees and beg, but my pride—okay, and respect for Ashley— prevent me from doing so.

I release a huff. "Fine. We'll meet at eleven."

"Sounds good." She leans over and kisses Cruz's temple, causing him to grumble in his sleep, before standing.

"Where's mine?" I hear myself asking, my words shocking me as much as they do her.

"You get a handshake." She sticks out her hand. "Gotta keep things professional and shit, right?"

The easy way she takes my blunder and makes a joke from it has me laughing. I take her hand and yank her into me, wrapping her in a hug—a friendly hug.

For a moment, with her in my arms and her head to my chest, all feels right, like I've found a piece of myself I never knew was missing. "See you tomorrow, Ash."

She pulls away. "See you tomorrow." And then, she's gone.

***

Cruz and I both are usually up before the sun rises. Except today, when I peel my eyes open, I find my little guy curled up on top of the covers beside me fast asleep.

I'm struck by how small he looks, with his knobby knees pulled to his chest and his hands tucked beneath his cheek. His breathing is deep and even as he peacefully slumbers.

How he snuck into my bed without me noticing is beyond me, but the fact that he came to me, that he felt safe with me, is something I'll treasure always.

This kid is everything I didn't know I needed, and I know beyond a shadow of a doubt, I'll fight tooth and nail for him should it come down to it.

I keep still instead of starting my morning routine, content merely watching him sleep. Eventually, he begins to stir, slowly blinking awake.

"G'morning, Daddy." His already raspy voice is thick with sleep.

"Good morning, bud. Did you sleep good?"

Sitting up, he wipes his eyes. "I had a bad dream."

"About what?"

"Mom."

"What about her?" I ask, keeping my voice calm even though my blood feels like lava, burning and bubbling angrily in my veins.

"She t-took me away. Away from you and Ashley."

This is one of the first times he's initiated a conversation with me, and the only time I've ever heard him call her by name, and it's tainted by Kelsey and the fear she instilled in him when she should have been his number one protector.

"It was only a dream, bud."

"B-but could it happen? Could she take me away?"

I open my arms to him, and he curls into my side, laying his head on my chest. "She might try." He whimpers, and my heart breaks. I swear on all that's holy, if Kelsey comes back, I'll call in every single favor I'm owed to combat her. "But I promise you—"

"Cross your heart promise?" he asks.

Nodding, I take his hand in mine and trace an X over my heart. "I cross my heart promise, I will do everything I can to keep you. You're my heart, dude. I love you."

"I love you, too, Daddy. A whole lot."

CHAPTER 26
ASHLEY

enny's is packed to the gills when I arrive. The lobby is shoulder-to-shoulder and there's a line on the sidewalk. I get it, though—Benny's food is kind of like a religious experience.

I spot Colton at a table in the back, but a familiar head of red hair stops me in my tracks. "Stacia!"

She whirls around, her son on her hip. "Hey, girl! What's up?"

"Just feeding the addiction you created."

"It has to be something in the powdered sugar." She shifts Asher up a little higher. "Are you here alone?"

I toe at the floor. "I'm meeting Colton and Cruz, actually."

"Oh, are you now?" She taps her husband on the shoulder, bringing him into our conversation. "Lookie who's here to meet Colton."

West smirks. "Imagine that."

The two exchange one of those married-couples-only looks before breaking out into matching grins. I don't know what I missed, but it feels huge.

"Is he here already?" Stacia asks.

"Yup, right back there." I incline my head toward his table. "Y'all wanna join us?"

"And skip this line?" West chuckles. "Yes, yes we do."

The four of us skirt the hostess and join Colton and Cruz. Luckily, he scored one of the coveted oversized booths.

When Asher catches sight of Cruz, he wriggles in his mom's arms until she sets him down, allowing him to make a mad dash for his friend. "Cruz!"

Colton looks up from his phone at the commotion. "Oh, hey."

"I brought friends," I say with a little shrug. He's so mercurial, even with his best friend, that I'm not sure how he will react.

"The more the merrier," he says, sounding surprised but not displeased as he slides out of the booth and gestures for me to sit between him and Cruz.

Asher, with assistance from Stacia, climbs into their side, scooting all the way down so he and Cruz can play.

None of us bother with a menu; it's French toast or bust, which makes ordering incredibly easy.

"How is the bad bride sitch?" Stacia asks, blowing on her coffee.

"She's been quiet for the last two weeks. Honestly, I think she's moved on from tormenting me."

"Thank God!" Stacia lifts her palms to the ceiling, lifting her shoulder. "Wait! Does that mean y'all are together now?"

"We're—"

Cruz cuts me off. "Agent Purple is gonna be my stepmom!"

Both Colton and I choke—him on coffee, and me on air, all the while wishing for the floor to split open and swallow me whole. Naturally, the married couple across from us finds this absolutely hilarious.

"Because you're our family. Right?" Cruz adds, his voice so full of hope.

"Bud," I start, but Colton thankfully takes over.

"Ashley is Daddy's friend. She's your friend, too. And sometimes, friends are like family, too. But that's all she is—a friend."

Ouch. While his explanation is accurate it stings. A lot.

Cruz looks to me, his eyes begging me to refute his father's words. I try to swallow, but it's like my mouth is full of sawdust. I reach over to Cruz and clasp his hand in mine, hoping the physical contact will soften my words. "Your daddy is right, 005. I'm a friend—but not just *any* friend. Your very best one."

Cruz shakes his head. "Nope. You'll see. I'm right. I know I am."

I can't help but smile at my determined little friend. Maybe he's got a sixth sense, too.

Clearly feeling we need a subject change, West asks, "Have you heard anything else from social services?"

Colton's mouth is too full of French toast to answer. He waves his fork in the air, signaling his friend to wait. After swallowing, he says, "Now that paternity has been established, they don't have much to do. Our social worker mentioned a friendly check-in just to make sure Cruz is adjusting, but otherwise, we're free and clear."

"Right on, man." West holds out his fist for Colton to bump.

The rest of our meal goes smoothly, with no more

talk of my and Colton's relationship—or lack thereof—and once everyone is finished, Colton invites the Larson family to join us at the kids' museum.

The museum is tucked away in an old brick building on the fringe of the downtown area. Cruz and Asher walk hand-in-hand up the ramp and into the building.

Asher tries making a beeline for the gift shop, his eyes on the display of stuffed animals. West intercepts him just before he crosses the threshold, scooping him up into his arms. The toddler whines, canting his body toward the plush animals. "After, mini-man. We can look after."

The little cutie thinks over his dad's offer and finally nods. "After."

We get in line for tickets before taking the elevator to the second floor. I'm not sure what I was expecting the museum to be like, but I can safely say, what greets us when we exit the elevator car isn't it.

It's more of a playhouse than a museum. The floor is split into four rooms, with a wide hallway. Each room is home to a different activity; there's a classroom, a grocery store, a Lego room, and a dinosaur dig. The hallway also offers a few activities as well, like magnet fishing and a reading area.

The boys flit from room to room, loading their shopping carts and building towers. They play for hours while West, Stacia, Colton, and I congregate in the hallway, keeping an eye on them and chatting while they play.

Eventually, Cruz and Asher wear themselves out and we head out—stopping by the gift shop, as promised—and go our separate ways, with plans in place to make this a monthly thing.

CHAPTER 27
COLTON

'm relaxing on the couch, having a nightcap, when my phone rings. An unexplainable thrill runs through me as I rush to answer without checking the screen.

"Hello." My voice comes out lower than usual.

"Colty, are you okay?" Disappointment chased by guilt flows through me. A small part of me hoped it was Ashley, even though I saw her only hours ago when I picked Cruz up. "You sound like you're coming down with something."

"I'm good," I assure her. "How are you?"

"No, no. A mother knows these things. What's going on?"

I've never been able to get away with shit; Mama Mel always knows.

"Mel—"

"Don't you Mel me, boy. Who is she? Is it the purple-haired girl my grandson is so smitten with?"

I answer with a long-suffering sigh rather than

words. Which is apparently all the confirmation Mama Mel needs.

"That's what I thought." She clucks her tongue. "When are you gonna bring her and that grandson of mine to see your Mama K and me?"

"Whoa, whoa. Slow down."

"Speed up! You're knocking on thirty's door and still single. When I was your age, Kim and I already had you—"

"I've got the kid!" I say, hating the whining edge in my voice.

"But not the girl," she fires right back.

An odd sensation settles over me with her words. Something a lot like loneliness, which is preposterous. I've never felt lonely before—and I've certainly never lacked for companionship. Except now, I only seem to want it from one woman—and there's still so much murkiness there that I can't seem to force myself to make a move.

"Bring her. You, Cruz, and the girl. Next weekend."

"She might have a wedding to shoot," I say, lamely.

"Then come during the week. Ain't nobody getting married on a weekday."

"I have court."

"Colton Elliot Banks! You stop making excuses, find a date, and bring your people to meet your mothers. Do you hear me?"

I puff out a resigned breath, knowing she won't let up until I agree. "Yeah, Mama Mel, I hear you. I'll text you a date."

"Such a good boy." I can practically hear her smile. "Love you."

"Love you, too." I end the call and promptly text Ashley.

> **ME**
>
> I have a question for you.

ASHLEY

Hmm. Sounds ominous.

> **ME**
>
> Tell me the worst thing you think it could be, then when it isn't anywhere near that bad, you'll feel relieved.

ASHLEY

But what if it's worse?

> **ME**
>
> It won't be.

ASHLEY

Fine. Worst case, you ask me to stay away from Cruz.

> **ME**
>
> Quite the opposite, actually. How would you feel about joining Cruz and me at the beach for a little getaway?

ASHLEY

Oh, um, wow. Like a day trip?

> **ME**
>
> More like a few days...
>
> To my moms' place.

> Mama Mel all but said your presence is mandatory, so please say yes? For me. And Cruz. And Mama Mel. You wouldn't want to upset an old lady.

> And maybe don't tell her I called her old?

Fuck. This—this right here—is what Ashley Murphy does to me. She makes me crazed and needy and willing to beg. I've never begged for a thing in my life—I've fought tooth and nail for the things I have, for the friendships I have.

And yet, here I am, begging her to accompany me to the beach. To meet my mothers. I can't decide if I've just hit a new low or if it's merely a side effect of *her.*

God knows, the woman needs a warning label: *Hot as hell; prolonged exposure may lead to distracting thoughts, an abundance of lust, and a deep-seated desire for commitment. Proceed with caution.*

ASHLEY

When?

ME

When are you free?

She sends me some dates and we firm up our plans to head down to Dogwood three weeks from now. Something tells me I'm going to be counting the days like a child waiting for Christmas.

As Cruz and I drive over to Ashley's to pick her up, I can't help but wonder for the millionth time what kind of swimsuit she's packed. I'm crossing my fingers for small, stringy, and skimpy, even though I know it won't be. At least not in front of Cruz and my moms.

A guy can dream though, right?

She's waiting on her porch with her bag at her side when we pull up. I shift my BMW into park and step out to greet her.

She bounds my way, and without a thought, I pull her into a hug as soon as she's within reach.

We both tense as my arms wrap around her, but I band them there and hold her close. "Ready to go?"

We're so close she has to tip her head back to look me in the eye. "As ready as ever."

Reluctantly, I release her and bend to retrieve her bag. I pop the trunk and stow it before helping her into the passenger seat. As she lowers herself into the seat, her linen shorts ride up, revealing more of her toned thighs.

The sight of her creamy thighs has me leaning into the car for a closer look. I play off my creepiness by pulling the seat belt across her with jerky movements.

I know I've made a mistake the second my fingers brush over her breasts. She sucks in a sharp breath, her eyes flying to mine in question, but I stay my course, dragging the belt over her hips to secure the buckle.

"Thanks," she whispers on a shaky exhale.

"No problem," I tell her, even though it most definitely is, because unless a miracle occurs on my short walk to the driver's side, I'll be starting this trip with some goddamn blue balls.

No miracle occurred and the first half of the drive was a special kind of hell. Sure, my boner deflated, but I still ached for release, to spill myself into the little temptress to my right.

Luckily, she struck up a game of I-Spy with Cruz, effectively halting all thoughts of sex. West wasn't kidding when he said nothing halts your arousal more than the sound of your kid's voice.

About an hour into the four-hour drive, Cruz conks out, leaving Ashley and me to speak a little more freely.

"I've been watching your accounts; it seems like Bridezilla is gone for good."

"Yup. All quiet. Oh, hey, you need to invoice me for your time and whatnot."

I choke out a laugh. As if I'm going to charge her for sending a letter after all she's done to help me with Cruz...*fat fucking chance.*

"I'm serious, Colton. You provided a service, and I need to pay you."

Her words are completely innocent, but my mind wanders to dark and dirty places. I'd love nothing more than to describe to her all of the services she could provide for me—in great detail.

"We'll see." I wave my right hand in a dismissive

gesture before resting it on the center console dangerously close to Ashley's left.

We talk about everything and nothing, bickering and bantering until finally, sleep takes her, too, leaving me with only my thoughts for the rest of the drive.

CHAPTER 28
ASHLEY

blink awake right as we come to a stop outside of the cutest beach house to ever exist. The two-story home is painted a catching shade of jade, with thick white trim and a driftwood gray wraparound porch. An inviting two-seater swing hangs facing the beach, which is across the street. It's the perfect spot to curl up with a book and an ice-cold drink.

I vow here and now to do just that at least once before we leave.

"Ashley." Colton says my name softly. I roll my head across the seatback to face him. "Oh, you're awake. Good. We're here."

"It's a beautiful house."

"It is. The whole area is great. I was hesitant to have my moms so far, but one visit and I knew it would be fine."

I unbuckle and step out of the car, breathing in the salty air. Colton follows suit.

"My best friend actually lives not too far from here."

"Oh, yeah? Where?"

"About an hour down the coast, in Bay Ridge."

"Maybe we can meet up with"—he hesitates—"her?"

I can't help my disbelieving laugh. "Why, Colton, are you fishing?"

Swear to glob, his cheeks turn pink. "Whatever. If you don't want to make plans—"

"Slow your roll. I never said that. I'll text her in a bit."

He leans back into the car and kills the engine, and then pops the trunk. "You want to get Cruz, and I'll get our stuff?"

"Sounds good." I pull the lever to tilt my seat forward so I can reach Cruz. "Hey, bud, wake up. We're here."

He jerks up in the seat, his small fists scrubbing at his eyes. "The beach? We're at the beach?"

"Yeah, it's right across the street. You wanna see?"

Cruz nods and I lean to unbuckle him. I step back, giving him room to climb out before taking his hand and walking him to the end of the driveway. "See?"

The view is like a painting—too pretty to be real. The narrow street gives way to grassy sand dunes. Beneath the dunes is a vast expanse of beach, with sand as white as sugar. The sound of soft waves breaking at the shore's edge mingles with the squawks of the seagulls and the laughs of mid-day beach goers. In short, it's paradise.

"It's so...big," Cruz says in awe. "The water looks like it goes forever."

Looking down at him, I nod. "It does look like that, huh?"

"You two coming? We can hit the beach first thing tomorrow. If I know my moms, they have plans for us today and are most likely taking turns watching us from the window."

"You ready to meet your grandmothers?" I ask.

Cruz shrugs and looks down.

"Your daddy and I will be with you the whole time. You've talked to them on the phone and on video chat. Don't be scared."

"I'm not." He puffs out his little chest. "I'm Agent 005, and I'm n-not scared of nothing."

"Such a brave boy. Let's go."

We catch up to Colton on the porch, where he has our bags arranged neatly by size. "Knock, knock," he says, opening the door without actually knocking.

"Colty!" a loud, boisterous voice calls out. My head whips toward the source, which, much to my surprise, is a little wisp of a woman. She has jet black hair that's nearly as long as she is tall, striking emerald eyes, bow-shaped lips, and deeply bronzed skin. She's breathtaking.

"Hey, Mama Mel," Colton says, bending to kiss her cheek.

"Oh, and what am I, chopped liver?" comes a second voice.

This must be Mama K, and while equally beautiful, she is her wife's polar opposite. She's tall and sturdy, with skin the color of freshly fallen snow. Her platinum hair is cropped close in a trendy pixie cut, and she has thick, red-framed glasses perched on her nose.

Truly, the only thing they have in common, outwardly, is their matching technicolor maxi dresses.

"Never, Mama K." He hugs her and kisses her cheek as well.

The only thing I can think upon seeing the bright,

vibrant women who raised my soulmate is how in the hell did he get so uptight?

I stand back while Colton introduces Cruz to his grandmothers. He surprises us both when he takes to them instantly.

"And you must be Ashley," the one he calls Mama Mel says. She rakes her gemstone gaze over every ounce of me—twice—before nodding. "Oh, yes, she'll do just fine," she says to her wife out of the side of her mouth. I'm fairly certain she didn't mean for me to hear her, but I did, and now I have a million questions bombarding me. The main one being—*I'll do just fine for what?*

"Nice to meet you." I offer her my hand.

"Nonsense, girl." She pulls me into a hug. Her head comes to my shoulder, but her grip rivals that of her son. I'm pretty sure she is the woman who inspired the phrase *small but mighty.* "And you can call me Mel—or Mama Mel, whichever. After all, we're family."

"Let the girl breathe," the taller woman tuts, pulling her wife away from me. "The name's Kim, dear, and it's a pleasure to meet you."

"Y'all as well. Your home is beautiful," I say, meaning it. The inside is every bit as bright as its occupants' personalities, and yet, it's soothing at the same time.

"And a charmer, too," Mel says, wagging her brows before turning to Cruz. "Would you like to see your room?"

His eyes widen in wonder. "I have my own room?"

"Well, of course you do!" She leans in conspiratorially and stage whispers, "And guess what?"

"What?"

"It has bunk beds!"

"For really real?"

She offers him her hand, which he eagerly takes, and together they set off to see his room. It's amazing what eight weeks of love and security can do for a child. While he still has a ways to go, he's really come into his own under Colton's care.

"We put y'all in the blue room," Kim says, as if it's no big deal.

"Us?" Colton asks. "In one room? Together?"

"I'm afraid so. The green room is under construction at the moment and out of use." She gives her son an indiscernible look. "Surely that's not a problem. After all, the bed is plenty big."

I swallow harshly at her words, coughing on air—which is nothing compared to Colton's reaction. He looks positively ready to wring her neck.

"Bed. *The.* Bed. As in there's only one?"

"Oh, Colton, hush. Surely you slept with a woman before."

"I'm booking a hotel."

He pulls his phone from his pocket, but Kim smacks it to the floor. I am riveted by the show in front of me—no one talks to Colton like this. I want popcorn.

"You will do no such thing. It'd break Mel's heart. Cruz's, too; did you see the way he lit up at the mention of bunkbeds?"

"Mama K—"

"It's been months since you've visited and now you want to book a hotel." She paces the length of the foyer and she rants, laying on the mom-guilt with the precision of a surgeon wielding a scalpel. "To think, you finally give us a grandchild to spoil, and you want to whisk him away to some big-chain-corporate hotel, when he could be here, bonding with his family."

He says her name again, but it's no use. He looks to me for help, which only serves to turn her attention my way as well.

"If I were young and single and someone told me I had to share a bed with a knockout like her…only a fool would say no." She whirls to glare at her son. "And I know I didn't raise no fool."

"Sorry, Mama K. The blue room is fine."

She flashes a blinding, victorious smile. "I knew you'd see it my way."

He huffs out a laugh. "Somehow, everyone always does."

She pats his cheek affectionately. "Why don't y'all go freshen up while I start dinner? We'll eat at five."

"Sounds great," he tells her, the expression on his face conveying his ambivalence as he bends to collect our bags.

"It was, uh, nice to meet you," I say, trying to remember my manners. Even though manners are the last thing on my mind after having the single-bed-bomb dropped on me. Suddenly, I'm super regretting the jammies I packed.

Various possibilities of how he'll react to my little silky lace-trimmed shorts and matching bralette race through my mind. *Will he like the way they look? Will they turn him on? Will he not react at all?* I'm not sure which option is worse.

"You as well, dear. You as well." She winks at me as if we're in on some great joke together, before turning and heading, presumably, into the kitchen.

Colton shoulders open the blue room only to stop in the entryway, causing me to walk into him. "Ouch! What the hell?"

I rub my forehead where it smacked into his strong back. As pretty as his body is to ogle, it freaking hurts in a head-on collision.

"Oh, come on!" he growls, his voice a mixture of upset and despair.

"What? What is it?"

He turns to me with a grim look on his handsome face. "See for yourself."

Colton steps into the room, allowing me entry. I immediately pinpoint the source of his frustration: the bed. The *very small* bed. I'm pretty sure Cruz's bed is larger than this one. It wouldn't surprise me if my feet dangle over the edge—it's that small.

"Could be worse."

He trains his glare on me now. "Could it, Ashley? How?"

I shrug. "Could be a futon."

With a growl, he drops our bags to the floor, grumbling under his breath all the while.

"Look, if it's that big of a deal, I'll bunk with Cruz. Your mom said he had bunk beds." Much to my annoyance, a hint of hurt seeps into my tone.

But his vehement displeasure over sharing a bed with me grates. It's not like I'm going to throw myself at him—*been there, got rejected, have no plans of trying again.*

"No, Ash. I'm sorry. I'm being dramatic. It's fine."

"Are you sure?"

"I'm sure. Trust me when I say those bunk bed mattresses are the worst; I couldn't subject you to them."

I nibble my lower lip, weighing my options. "Are you super sure?"

Colton's lips quirk into a half smile as he draws an X over his heart. "Cross my heart."

"All right," I say on a yawn. "How long until dinner?"

"It's three-thirty now, so an hour and a half."

"There's something about car rides that just zaps my energy."

He nods like he knows what I mean.

"Would you—and your moms—mind if I went out to the porch swing and read for a bit?"

"Not one bit. I'm gonna go check on Cruz."

I grab my Kindle and we head back downstairs together, going our separate ways at the bottom. I venture into the kitchen in search of a drink before heading outside.

The fragrant aroma of garlic hits me before I reach the kitchen. And sure enough, Kim is standing with her back to me, busy at work in front of the stove. Without ever taking her eyes off of her pan, she somehow knows it's me.

"There's lavender lemonade in the fridge, Ashley. Beer, too. Glasses are in the china cabinet."

"Um, thank you," I say, hoping my confusion doesn't come across as rudeness.

"You're quite welcome."

Lavender lemonade in one hand and my Kindle in the other, I make my way out to the porch swing.

I admire the sunset as I sip my drink before diving head first back into my latest read—a ridiculously hilarious romantic comedy about a divorced couple remarrying Vegas style after a night of drinking. I'm still at the start of the book, and the heroine, Nya, has just woken up the morning after, clad in tulle with a new shiny rock on her finger.

Her panic is almost palpable as she pieces it all together. And her banter with her hot-as-sin ex-husband has me grinning like a loon. Before I know it, the sun has dipped low enough to kiss the water and dinner is ready.

CHAPTER 29
COLTON

Dinner is both torture and rapture. Mama K went all out for dinner and made her famous sticky ribs with garlic mac-n-cheese and homemade fries.

But with every bite, Ashley makes these happy little moans. And don't even get me started on the finger licking. *Goddamn, the finger licking.* If I have to watch her suck the barbecue sauce from her fingers one more time, I won't be held responsible for my actions.

She's a temptress of the highest order. Everything the woman does screams of sex. And she doesn't even mean to do it. I feel like I'm on the verge of madness.

Which is why I'm pointedly ignoring her, giving all of my focus to Mama Mel and Cruz while Ashley chats up Mama K. Or trying to ignore her anyway.

"Will I see a shark?" Cruz asks excitedly, drawing my attention back to him.

"At the beach?" Mama Mel chortles. "I hope not."

"Oh." My son pouts down at his plate. "What about an octopus?"

"Probably not, bud." He looks crushed, and I hate it.

"But I know where you can see them," I rush to add.

"Where? Can we go?" His excitement pinches at my heart.

"The aquarium. I'm sure we can find one within driving distance."

Mama K claps excitedly, getting everyone's attention. "You're in luck, boy. They just opened one up not too far from here, in Bay Ridge."

Ashley's eyes light up. "My best friend lives there. We planned on making a trip to see her."

"There ya go," Mama Mel says before turning back to Cruz. "How would you feel about building a pillow fort in your room after dinner?"

"I've never built a fort before." He looks to me for my approval, and I nod. "Let's do it!"

Once everyone is stuffed, Ashley offers to do the dishes, but Mama K politely tells her guests don't do housework. Ashley tries to argue, but Mama K is a force to be reckoned with and shuts her down.

"Why don't you kids take a walk or watch a movie—the night is young."

I look to Ashley, silently asking her what she'd like to do.

"A walk sounds nice."

"Perfect," Mama K says, sounding far too excited. "Y'all take a little moonlight stroll, and we'll see y'all in the morning. Breakfast is at eight. Be here or be hungry."

I wait on the porch, enjoying the balmy night air, while Ashley runs upstairs for her sweater. I was a little anxious about bringing her here, about having her meet my mothers, but it was wasted worry.

I can't deny the sense of rightness thrumming through me right now. Mama K and Mama Mel took an instant liking to her—just like Cruz did. It seems as though I'm the only one who wasn't roped in at first sight.

But that's not really true. As much as I denied it, I was completely enraptured by her smooth skin and green eyes. I fought my attraction to her pouty lips and sharp tongue, tooth and nail. I told her, myself, and anyone that would listen that she wasn't my type. Which is true—I've always gone for docile and petite women—arm candy, if you will.

But Ashley…she has a fire to her, and as much I keep fighting it, I kind of like the burn.

"You ready?" Ashley asks from behind, causing me to snap to attention.

I tip my head toward the beach and start walking. We leave our shoes at the bottom of the dunes and head to the shoreline.

"How often do you visit?"

A sigh escapes my lips as I press them into a thin line. "Not often enough. Though, I suppose Cruz will change that."

Ashley kicks at the water, sending droplets into the air. "That's good. He needs people who love him in his life."

I grunt noncommittally, even though she's right.

"You're a good dad, you know that, right?"

"Am I? Some days I don't know. This has been a lot of catch-up, all very fast."

She grabs my hand and stops suddenly. "Look at me." She pulls me toward her and I spin to face her, struck by how absolutely gorgeous she looks in the moonlight. "You are exactly what he needed. You stepped up to the plate when a lot of men wouldn't have. You're kind and caring and compassionate, and patient with him. You make him feel safe and show him every day how much you love him. Cut yourself some slack, Colton, because as far as I can see, you're rocking the dad thing."

"Thanks." My voice is stiff even to my own ears. "I appreciate it."

"You're so uptight," Ashley says with a shake of her head, her laughter cutting through the night air like music made only for me.

Even as she laughs at my expense, I find myself wanting nothing more than to kiss her.

"I'm not that uptight," I defend, turning slightly away from her to look out at the calm water.

"Oh, yeah? Have you ever skinny dipped?"

I whip my head around to look at her, only to find her shirt discarded at her feet and her hands on the clasp of her bra. "What are you doing?" I hiss.

She lets her bra drop, revealing her perky B-cups to me. They're high and firm on her chest, a perfect handful.

"Ashley!" Her name leaves my lips in an urgent plea. Though, I'm not sure if I'm trying to get her to stop taking her clothes off or if I'm begging her to remove them faster.

"Colton," she says my name back with a teasing lilt as she shimmies out of her shorts and panties and takes off into the water. "Are you coming? The water feels great!"

I watch, with a small smile on my lips, as she

splashes and frolics in the water without a care in the world. And then, against all better judgment, I strip down and run in after her.

"You little liar!" I holler as my balls recede, seeking the warmth of my body. "The water is fucking freezing!"

"Feels fine to me." She shrugs, the moonlight casting her in an almost ethereal glow. "Maybe you should swim a little bit closer?"

We're playing a dangerous game, and I know good and well getting any closer to her while we're both naked won't lead to anywhere good. Or rather, it will be *too* good. I should turn around and swim toward the shore. I should get dressed, and demand she do the same, and then I should bunk down with Cruz.

And yet, I find myself paddling out, diving head first into the temptation that is Ashley Murphy.

"See?" she says once I'm standing before her. "Isn't that better?" We're out far enough that the water covers us both from the chest down, but the memory of her naked body bathed in moonlight is permanently etched into my mind.

The water feels the same, but the thought of my little temptress's bare skin so close to mine has my body temperature—and my cock—rising.

"You're crazy, you know that?" I ask.

"Is that a bad thing?" she fires right back, splashing a little water my way.

I pretend to mull over her question. "Hmmm."

"Jackass!" She slices her hands through the salty water, sending a surge my way.

"You're gonna pay for that, devil woman!"

"Gotta catch me first!" She dives headlong into the surf and, like the sucker I am, I give chase.

Even with her head start, I'm on her in two strides. I band my arms around her from behind, pinning her back to my chest. "Gotcha!" I whisper into her ear, before skimming my nose down the column of her neck.

She inhales sharply. "Colton."

"Do you know what you do to me?" I speak the words against her skin, peppering her neck and shoulder with kisses between words.

"Tell me." She arches her back, and I skim my hands up to cup her breasts.

"You make me feel wild." I tweak and tug at her stiff nipples. "Reckless."

A soft moan slips past her parted lips as she tips her head back onto my shoulder, looking up at with me with wanton desire in her eyes. "Is that a bad thing?"

"I've always been risk averse." I hold her tighter to me with my left hand while I slide my right hand down between the valley of her breasts. She trembles in my arms as I drag my fingertips over the lean lines of torso, not stopping until I'm cupping her pussy. The warmth of her arousal is a stark contrast to the cool water surrounding us. "But you…"

"Me?" She rolls her hips as I explore her folds, applying pressure to her clit with the heel of my hand.

"You make me want to risk it all." I drive two fingers into her as I claim her lips, swallowing down any reply she might have had.

"Oh, fuck," she moans as she rocks against me, the waves around us setting our tempo.

"That's right, Ash," I groan my praise, "show me how much you want it."

I fuck her with my fingers, murmuring all sorts of

filthy promises in her ear, until she completely falls apart in my arms beneath the light of the moon.

No sooner than she comes down from her release does she start shivering. "Come on, Ash. Let's head back."

"What about you?"

"Next time," I tell her with a wink.

CHAPTER 30
ASHLEY

We race back along the shore, up the dunes, and across the street to Colton's moms' house. We're both covered in sand and shivering by the time we make it back.

"Leave your shoes," he whispers, toeing his off. I follow suit and then we slip inside and up the stairs.

"S-s-so cold." My teeth chatter.

"I'll warm you up." Colton grabs my hand, pulling me along behind him and into the bathroom. He flips the lock on the door and starts the shower, fiddling with the temperature before turning to me. "Ditch the clothes."

He strips out of his own shirt before shucking off his shorts and boxers.

The chills wracking my body turn to a different kind of quake as I take in his naked form. Even in the harsh bathroom light, he's a solid ten. Long and lean, firm and sculpted, his body is the kind photographers beg to shoot. He's a modern-day Renaissance sculpture come to life—except with a much bigger dick.

When I don't move immediately—far too busy staring at his sinewy muscle wrapped in supple golden skin to worry about being cold—he reaches out and tugs on the ends my hair. "Come on. Let's get you warmed up."

I shake out of my fog and strip. "Thanks."

He holds the curtain back, letting me step under the spray first. "Oh, that feels so good," I moan as the warm water cascades over me.

"Bet I can make you feel better." He backs me into the cold tile wall, but his body offers all the heat I need.

"I'm not fucking you in your moms' house," I hiss.

"You're right. We're not fucking. Because when I'm inside of your tight, hot pussy for the first time, it'll be in my bed, and you'll be begging me for it."

Colton drops to his knees, licking his lips as he looks up at me.

"Then what are you doing?"

"Eating my dessert." He runs his hands up and down my legs a few times. "Put your foot on the bench."

I comply as he holds me steady.

"Such a pretty pussy." He leans forward and licks me from bottom to top, flicking my clit with the tip of his tongue before pulling away. "I've been dying to taste you for weeks. Dreaming of it, jacking off to thoughts of it."

Feeling emboldened by his words, I reach down and run my fingers through my wetness. "And? Is it everything you imagined?"

"More," is all he says before burying his face in my pussy and devouring me whole. He licks and sucks and slurps as he moves his fingers deep inside of me, curling them to hit that sweet spot until I'm falling apart for him—because of him—for the second time tonight.

But this time, I'm not content to be the only one satisfied. When he stands, with a pleased smirk on his face, I drop to my knees and flip the switch, taking him into my mouth before he can utter a single word.

I take him as deep as I can before sliding my lips back up the length of him. He gathers my wet, salt-tangled hair in his hands and tugs until my eyes meet his.

A strangled groan lodges in his throat as I dive back down on his dick, sucking and licking. In no time, he's fucking my face in earnest, all the while telling me how good my mouth feels and how he can't wait to experience the real thing.

I can tell he's close when his hips start bucking and his pace falters. Wanting to blow his mind the way he did mine, I reach up and cup his balls, massaging them in time with his thrusts.

He groans and taps my cheek. "Going to come."

I suck harder, giving him the proverbial all clear. He pumps once…twice…three times more before he pins me in place with my forehead flush to his abdomen as he shoots his load.

"Fuck," he groans shakily as I pull my mouth away and spit his come to the shower floor.

"You okay?" I ask, wiping my mouth with the back of my hand.

He slides down the wall to the shower floor. "I think you broke me."

I lean forward and press a kiss to the corner of his mouth. "No, Colt, I blew you."

"That you did, body and mind." He scrubs his hands

over his face. "If oral with you is that good, I-I think sex might kill me."

I grin as I stand to my feet. "But what a way to go."

After we recover, we take turns washing up before heading back to the bedroom. Colton slides on a pair of fresh boxers while I change into my bralette and shorts set.

Upside to tonight's sexy shenanigans—I'm no longer nervous about him seeing me in the bedtime silk and lace.

He eyes me appreciatively as I climb into the bed, claiming the right side as mine.

"You know it's not even ten, right?"

I stretch my arms over my head, arching my back in a yawn. "Feels later. I'm exhausted."

He settles down beside me. "Then let's sleep."

Shockingly, there's no awkwardness as I lay my head on his chest and snuggle into his side. Nope, there's just an overwhelming sense of contentment. Of rightness. Like I'm exactly where I need to be.

CHAPTER 31
COLTON

For the first time in I don't know how long, I sleep in. Well, by my standards, anyway. And it's all thanks to the knockout of a woman sharing the bed with me.

We're still pressed together in the same position we fell asleep in, with her head on my chest. Only now, I have one arm beneath her, cradling her head, and the other wrapped around her, gripping her ass beneath the silk of her shorts, holding her to me. Our legs are intertwined, and there's not an inch of space between us.

Something about sleeping beside this woman soothes me; she quiets the chaos of my brain...my soul. Deep in the recess of my mind, there's a voice whispering to me that this is what true happiness feels like.

I ignore that little voice in favor of watching Ashley sleep. She looks so peaceful with her purple hair fanned out across the white sheets and her lips slightly parted. Her chest rises and falls in an even pattern with each breath. I almost wish I could freeze this moment, to remember the way I feel here and now, to hold on to it always.

You could have this always, the voice whispers to me, *you could have her for always, if you only stopped pushing her away.*

Ashley blinks herself awake, saving me from arguing with myself like a crazy person. And therein lies the problem—Ashley Murphy good and truly makes me crazy.

Though, the more time I spend with her, the more I find myself wondering if her brand of crazy is such a bad thing.

"Good morning, handsome," she murmurs, sleepily, gazing up at me from beneath her lashes. "What time is it?"

I glance to the clock on the nightstand. "A little after seven."

She makes the cutest sleepy noise as she stretches. "I could stay in this bed next to you forever." Her entire body stiffens, and she quickly tries back tracking. "Because you know, the bed. It's so comfortable. And don't get me started on these sheets—"

I silence her with a kiss, pressing my lips to hers. I kiss her thoroughly, leaving no doubt that I feel the same. But just in case, I break the kiss and give her my words, too. "I slept better than I ever have with you next to me." I peck at her lips again. "I could easily make a habit of sharing a bed with you."

"W-what?" she stammers, her voice equal parts pleased and confused.

"You heard me, Ash." I extricate myself from the tangled mess of sheets. "Don't fish for compliments; it's unbecoming."

She pouts and gives me puppy dog eyes, and when that doesn't work, she toys with the strap of her lacy bra-thing, sliding it down her shoulder, batting her lashes as she reveals the swell of her breast to me.

A weaker man would crumble under—*oh, who am I kidding*—I fall like a house of cards. "I slept better last night, with your body pressed into mine, than I ever have in my entire life." Viper-fast, I lean forward and steal one last kiss. "I'm gonna shower before breakfast. Join me or don't, it's up to you."

———

I'm mildly disappointed when Ashley doesn't join me in the shower, but at the same time, I get it. Fooling around in your man's moms' house under the cloak of night is way different than doing it in the daytime.

Not that I'm her man or anything…because I'm not. We're simply two adults engaging in a little bout of mutual pleasure.

I bang my head against the shower wall—the same one I ate her against last night—in defeat. Because that sounds like a load of shit, even to me.

When I step back into the bedroom, Ashley is dressed and ready for the day. Her gauzy coverup gives no hint at the type of swimwear lurking beneath, but I'm happy to let my imagination run wild.

"Miss me?" I ask, dropping my towel.

Her eyes widen, and she licks her lips. "I did, but you wanna know who I miss more?"

I bristle, wondering who in the hell my girl is missing. "Who?"

"Cruz."

Fuck and double fuck. Not only did I just call Ashley my girl, but hearing her prioritize my son over my dick…I think I just fell a little harder.

"Yeah, that's fair." I grab my swim trunks from my bag and slip into them. "Let's go see 005."

Ashley arches her brows at me. "Race you, Agent C!" She darts out of the room and down the stairs. I forgo a shirt and follow, hot on her heels, the two of us busting into the kitchen like the Kool-Aid man.

Three sets of eyes regard us: one in confusion, the other two in knowing delight.

"What's all the commotion?" Mama K asks, standing from her barstool to grab two mugs from the cabinet.

"Just excited to see my favorite dude." I walk over to my son and wrap him in a bear hug. "It was weird not seeing your face first thing."

"Gramma Mel said you and Agent Purple needed to sleep. She said y'all probably had a late night."

"No, Cruz, I said they had a *long* night." Her tone is upbeat and good-natured, which is why I don't see it coming. "I cleaned up all the water the two of you tracked in. I hope you enjoyed your *dip* in the gulf."

Ashley squeaks out an unintelligible sound, but I just groan. Ever since I was kid, I've never been able to get away with shit, so Mama Mel knowing—or at the very least, strongly suspecting—what we got up to last night doesn't surprise me in the least.

"Mel, let the kids be," Mama K admonishes her before focusing her attention on Ashley. "A little birdie told me you liked French toast."

"I do," Ashley replies, her cheeks the color of the red Fiestaware mug she's sipping coffee from.

"You haven't lived until you've had my caramel-soaked French toast. Sit, let me serve you."

And just like that, Ashley is swept up in Hurricane Kim.

In no time flat, a heaping plate of food is placed before her. Since my girl has an appetite, she digs in. "Oh, wow." She scarfs down two more bites. "That is divine."

"I helped!" Cruz says, standing tall.

Ashley smiles so big her nose scrunches. "That explains why it tastes so good."

Cruz drags his barstool closer to Ashley, seemingly as infatuated with her as I am.

We chat throughout the rest of breakfast about our plans for the day, deciding to beach it this morning and do a little shopping after lunch.

Two hours of sun and sand later, Cruz finally decides he's ready to brave the waters of the Gulf.

"You're sure a shark won't eat me, Daddy?"

I refuse to make promises to him that are beyond my control, so instead, I say, "I promise to stay right by your side and to never let you go, not even for a second."

He searches my face, smart enough to know I skirted around the shark issue.

"Agent Purple, will you come, too?"

Ashley hops up from where she's been reading on her towel. "Of course!" My eyes roam over her swimsuit appreciatively. For all my imagining, none of it prepared me for the real deal. She's not in a skimpy two piece—

hell, I can't even see her stomach—and somehow, she looks hotter than ever.

"Okay." He nods once. "Let's do this."

I hold his left hand and Ashley his right as we wade out into the surf. He whimpers when the first wave breaks, crashing against his knees, bringing with it seaweed and foam. With the second, he squeals. And the third—he laughs like a loon.

Before long, the three of us are trying to jump the waves. One a little bigger than the rest rolls in and sweeps Cruz's feet from beneath him, sending him face-first into the salty water.

I reach for him, panic gripping my chest. I expect tears, but instead he pops up sputtering but smiling. "Did"—he coughs up a little water— "did you see me go under water?"

Ashley rolls her lips inward to keep from laughing. "We did see you, bud. But maybe next time, plug your nose first."

He looks at her funny. "How do you do that?"

She spends the next forty minutes teaching him to hold his breath. He puts up a little fight when it's time to go, until Mama Mel tells him we're going out for lunch.

It looks like his grandmothers learned overnight what took me weeks—food is the way to my boy's heart.

My moms take us to a little local place called Dilly's for lunch. It's your typical small-town lunch spot, decorated with bright colors and a menu full of diner fare. We order a few appetizers for the table along with our drinks.

"So, bud, did you like the beach?" I ask my tired son. His eyelids are heavy, and he nearly fell asleep on the drive over.

"It was super awesome. I wanna go all the time."

"Good thing Gramma Mel and KK live here, huh?" Mama Mel asks. The bond my son and moms has formed in such a short time blows my mind. He almost took to them faster than he did to Ashley. "You're welcome to visit us anytime."

"Anytime?" he asks, his once-drooping eyes now wide open.

"That's right."

"And if your daddy doesn't wanna drive you," Mama K interjects, "we'll come get you."

"Overbearing woman," I mutter good naturedly, only for her to cuff me upside the back of my head.

"No back-talk from you, boy."

I roll my eyes, fighting a grin. "Yes, ma'am."

Ashley's noticeably quiet beside me, with her phone in her hands and her eyes glued to the screen. "You okay?" I ask her softly.

"Oh, yeah, sorry." She grins sheepishly. "I was texting Mally. Does tomorrow sound good for the drive out to Bay Ridge?"

"Sounds good." I knock my shoulder into hers, grinning. "I'm excited to meet your best friend. It's almost on par with you meeting my moms."

Her smile dims a little, and while I want to dig into why, the middle of a family lunch is not the time or place. "Hey, Cruz," I say, redirecting my attention, "we're going to go to the aquarium tomorrow!"

My little dude bounces in his seat, his excitement a live wire. "That's where the sharks are, right? And octopuses?"

"That's right, bud."

"Yes!" He throws his gangly arms in the air, celebrating like he scored a touchdown.

The rest of lunch flies by in a blur of fried food and soda refills. By the end of the meal, Cruz's tiredness is back and Mama Mel offers for her and Mama K to bring him home for a rest instead of shopping.

I know he's used to having quiet time when Ashley keeps him, so I readily agree. Not to mention, he'll get a little extra time with his grandmothers, and I'll get a little more alone time with a certain little temptress.

Sounds like a double-win to me.

ASHLEY

"Got anywhere you want to go?" Colton asks as we walk to his car.

"I need to grab a gift for Mally and Natalie."

"What kind of gift?"

"A baby gift," I reply, hoping Colton doesn't catch my wistful tone.

But he does. *Of course, he does.* "Do you want kids?"

"Glob, yes!" My cheeks burn. "You know, one day. In the future."

"Why do you do that?" he asks.

"Do what?"

"Say that—glob?"

I think I'd rather discuss kids. "Um, my grammy raised me, and I wasn't allowed to say 'God' at all, unless I was praying, so I started saying glob."

"You've never talked about her before…" he presses, expertly navigating us to whatever destination he has in mind.

I shrug. "Not much to say. She was a militant, mean old woman who died the day after I turned eighteen."

"Is, uh, is she your only family?"

"Yup," I pop the P, hating this conversation with every ounce of my being.

"I feel like I'm missing something. You're so carefree, vibrant, and spirited."

"Everything she wasn't. If Grammy would have had her way, I'd have gone to an all-girls school and wifed up after I graduated, if only to get me out of her perfectly set hair." I laugh darkly. "But there wasn't one in our area, and she couldn't afford to send me off. Our relationship was…tenuous, at best, borderline abusive at worst."

I lay my head against the cool glass of the car window. "I never really had any friends in high school, because she never let me go anywhere. After she died, I kind of went buck wild. I was young and didn't know myself. I'd only ever been the good, quiet girl she wanted me to be, so I cycled through every clique there was, every trend, every fad. I kind of just threw a bunch of personalities at the wall, and this is the one that stuck."

"How'd you end up taking pictures?"

"Luck?" I say it more like a question than an answer. "Somewhere between my hippie and artsy phases, a camera landed in my hand. And while I can't draw for shit, I really liked the way images spoke."

"You're meant for it," Colton says. "A natural."

"It took a lot of digging and a lot of practice, but I'm…thankful. It's funny, actually; the first person I ever took pictures of was Mally. We ended up as roomies, and she likes to say I saved her, but I think she saved me, too."

"What about…" He pauses, and I know what's coming. "Your parents?"

"They were both only children. They died when I was four in a wreck. I—I don't really even remember them."

Colton smoothly guides his car into a parking spot in front of a little strip of stores. Before I can speak, much less move, he has us both unbuckled and me wrapped in his arms. The center console digs into me, but I don't care, because the feeling of him holding me, consoling me, is *everything*.

I don't realize I'm crying until Colton releases me and wipes away my tears. "It's okay, you're okay. God, Ashley, you're strong and beautiful and funny and so damn kind."

"Thank you. Truly." I flip down the visor mirror and check my reflection—I'm no worse for wear, as my splotchy cheeks blend in with my slight sunburn. "Hey, while we're on the whole family thing, your moms…"

"Adopted me. My bio-mom is actually Mel's sister. She had cancer and chose to have me over treatment. She knew it would kill her, but she said I was worth it and had my adoption all set up before I was ever born."

My tears start anew. "Oh, Colt—I'm so sorry."

He gives me a wobbly grin. "Mama Mel and Mama K are all I've ever known. Mel's parents pretty much wrote her off when she came out, and they did the same with my bio-mom when she wouldn't abort me. I've never met them, and to be honest, I don't really want to."

Impulsively, I lean over to press a kiss to his lips. It's

a chaste kiss, over before it begins, but it's enough to comfort him and me both. "They don't know what they're missing."

"Damn right they don't." He winks before turning to exit the car.

I climb out after him, rounding the hood to meet him. "Where are we going?"

"Google said STORK was the best baby store around, and you need baby gifts, so yeah—here we are."

I'm touched by his thoughtfulness. I figured we'd hit up the nearest Target, not go to an upscale baby boutique. Then again, with Colton, I should have known better. From raising his son, to defending his clients, to orgasms, the man doesn't half-ass anything.

Baby fever hits me the second we step into the boutique, completely wiping out my lingering melancholy from our talk in the car. The space is artfully arranged, showcasing a variety of luxurious baby items. They have swaddles and quilts, teethers and rattles, as well as a small selection of gorgeous baby clothes.

The far end of the shop is divided into five small rooms, each one a different style nursery.

It's a little overwhelming, the wall-to-wall baby madness, but at the same time, I'm itching to explore it all. Glob knows how long it'll be until I have a baby of my own, so I might as well spoil my bestie and her babies until then.

I start at the front of the store, with Colton following dutifully behind me, holding all of my purchases while I shop. I grab two swaddles—one pink and one blue— along with two super-soft knotted gowns. I grab the matching hat and headband as well, along with two pacifiers.

"Okay! Now I just need something for Natalie's kids."

Colton's eyes bug out. "This is all for one kid?"

"First of all, you're hardly one to talk—do you remember Cruz's shopping trip? Second, Mally is having twins."

"Point made."

I smile at his concession before grabbing a Noodle and Boo gift set for Natalie's baby, along with a set of kid-friendly bath bombs for Tatum, her daughter.

"All set."

Honestly, I could spend a lot longer, perusing the displays, but my ovaries are practically raring to go, screaming Ricky Bobby style that *they wanna go fast!* Preferably with the man acting as my shopping cart.

I pay for my haul, and we stow my bags in Colton's car before checking out the other shops in the strip. We hit up the toy store and a bookstore for Cruz, as well as an arts and crafts store for me to restock.

"Hey, let's run in here really fast," Colton says, nodding toward a flower shop.

The door of the shop is rose-petal red and the word Stems is spelled across the glass insert in a green, vine-like script.

"Sure."

Inside, there is display after display of various bouquets. They range from simple to absolutely over the top, and I love them all. One of my favorite things about shooting weddings is the detail pics; there's something about capturing and highlighting the little details that might be forgotten twenty years down the road but meant so much on the day.

Not bothering to look around, Colton strolls straight

up to the counter and orders two bouquets—one for each of his mothers. With the florist's assurance they'll be delivered tomorrow, we decide to call it a day and head home.

CHAPTER 33
COLTON

After another long night spent worshiping Ashley with my fingers and tongue, I'm tempted to sleep in. But I've got a little work to do this morning before we head out to Bay Ridge, so I'm up at my normal time.

As much as it pains me to leave the warmth of the bed—and Ashley's body—I slide out from beneath the covers and quickly work through some stretches before hopping in the shower.

I turn the water to steaming and lather up. As I run my hands over my body, memories of all of the dirty things Ashley and I did in here together race to the forefront of my mind as my blood races straight to my dick. Squirting a little more soap into my hand, I get myself off under the hot spray, wishing like hell it was Ashley's sweet little pussy milking me and not my own two hands.

After my shower, I dress for the day and head downstairs. Mama K is already in the kitchen, a pot of coffee percolating while she fries up a pan of bacon.

"Morning," she says in greeting, passing me a mug.

"What are you making?"

"Just a little breakfast hash."

"Mm. Yum."

"I figured since that boy of yours is a good eater, he wouldn't mind the veggies."

I snort out a laugh. "You can thank Ashley for that."

"She has a way with him, huh?"

"That she does."

"So, when are you going to make it official?"

"Make what official?" I ask, parking myself at the island and pulling up my email.

"You and the girl. When are you going to, as they say, put a ring on it?"

"Mama K, I think you have the wrong idea about Ashley and me."

No, she doesn't, that stupid voice in the back of my mind whispers.

"I most certainly do not!" My mother looks downright affronted. "That girl is meant for you. It's painfully obvious to anyone with eyes." She cuts her eyes at me. "Except you, apparently."

"Tell me how you really feel, Mama K."

"Colty, you don't want to know how I really feel."

My stubbornness, which I come by honestly from the woman glaring at me across the kitchen, sinks its claws in. "I do. Tell me."

"You asked for it, boy.

"I think you have yourself a helluva sweet set-up, and you're too chicken-shit to try for more for fear you might ruin it. But what you forget is sometimes taking a chance—a risk—is the only way to get the reward."

"And you think Ashley's my reward?"

"I think she could easily be your queen, my sweet, foolish boy. The question is, are you willing to put in the work to woo her?"

Mama K turns her back to me, telling without words that our talk is over. I sift through a few emails, replying to the ones that require it and cataloging the rest into the proper folders so I don't lose them.

West has tried—countless times—to convince me to hire help, from bringing in a partner to a PA, but I'm not interested. I have my system down pat and have less than zero desire to teach it to someone new.

However, now that I have Cruz, I'm starting to wonder if the idea doesn't have some merit. At the least, an assistant would free up a little more time to spend with him.

At 7:15 a.m., Cruz and Mama Mel join us. Still half asleep, my little guy crawls into my lap. I hold him to my chest, rocking us both slightly. "You sleep good, 005?"

"Yeah, Daddy, but I'm real excited to see the sharks."

"We're going to head that way around lunchtime. Why don't you go watch some TV until breakfast is ready?"

He nods and takes off for the living room.

"How about you?" Mama Mel asks in his wake. "How did you sleep?"

For a split-second I worry she overheard what Ashley and I got up to, and maybe she did, but God knows, I'm smart enough not to admit guilt or self-incriminate. "Like a baby. That mattress was a solid investment."

Before either woman can reply, Ashley pads into the room, dressed in a loose-fitting jumpsuit with her long purple hair in a braid and her feet still bare. "Good morning," she chirps happily.

My eyes track her as she breezes into the room, helping herself to a cup of coffee before taking a seat on the stool next to me. Without thinking through the repercussions, I wrap my arm around her shoulders and press a kiss to her temple.

I don't think twice about it until I catch the look Mama Mel is shooting Mama K. They're having some kind of silent conversation—and Ashley and I are definitely the topic.

I have no regrets, though, because in truth, the idea of being able to touch her whenever the hell I like sounds like a damn dream come true.

After breakfast—which Cruz declares is his new favorite—I find myself on my own once again. Mama K and Mel took Cruz into the backyard to introduce him to the wonders of water gun art. It was one of my favorite things as a kid, and I love that my moms are passing it down to him. Ashley tagged along to snap some pics of the trio.

I use my free time to do something I never do—nap. I drift in and out of sleep on the couch as dreams of Ashley flash behind my lids. Dreams of her being Cruz's mom, and the three of us being one big happy family. It's funny, because two months ago, the thought of her being my anything would have been a nightmare.

The sound of knocking wakes me. I check my watch —right on time—and stretch before hauling myself up from the couch. I check the peephole on the door before venturing out back to get everyone.

"Someone knocked," I say loudly to be heard over Cruz's delighted laughter. It seems water gun painting has gotten an upgrade since I was kid. Whereas I had two or three dollar-store squirt guns and old bed sheets, my boy is equipped with Super Soakers and stretched canvases.

"Did you answer the door?" Mama K asks.

I shrug. "Not my house."

"Swear, it's like I didn't raise you with any manners," Mama K mutters, shooting daggers my way.

"Let's go see who's on the porch." Mama Mel says to her wife before turning to Cruz. "These can dry in the sun until we get home."

We all head inside and huddle around the front door. Mama K swings it open to reveal the three bouquets I ordered yesterday.

"Aren't these lovely." Mama Mel picks up the spray of white lilies first. She checks the name on the card and passes them to my other mother.

Then she grabs the bunch of multi-colored tulips, addressed to her, inhaling their fresh scent before placing them on the console table.

The final bouquet is made up of white roses, lavender waxflowers and addressed to none other than my little temptress. Mama Mel's eyes light up when she sees Ashley's name on the card.

She passes the ribbon-tied bundle to Ashley with a know-it-all grin plastered across her delicate features.

"Are these...for me?" Ashley asks, accepting the flowers.

"They are."

"You've really got a thing for flowers, huh?" She traps her lower lip between her teeth, and I have to clench my fists to keep from reaching out and freeing it.

Smirking, I tell her to read the card. I remember

verbatim the words I scrawled onto the piece of card-stock clutched between her slender fingers.

Ashley,

I don't know what this thing is between us, but I want to explore it. I want to see what we could be if given the chance. So, please, even though I'm undeserving, give me a chance.

-Colton

Nausea rolls through me as she reads the card. Once, twice, three times. "Are you"—her voice pitches higher —"punking me?"

Uncaring that we have an audience, I step up to her and take the flowers from her grip, laying them on the table beside the tulips. "Not punking you, Ash. I meant every word."

Her eyes are glistening but her smile is bright as she nods.

"Is that a yes? Are you going to give me a chance? I want your words."

"Yeah." Another nod. "Yes."

I skim my knuckles along her jawline, feeling like I just won the damn Powerball. "Good."

"But, Colton—" She says my name with a hint of warning in her voice. "If you hurt me, I'll make you regret it tenfold. And," she leans in to whisper in my ear, "if we don't work out, prepare for me to stick around, because I'm not abandoning Cruz."

If I wasn't already half in love with her, I sure as hell am now. Her fierce protectiveness of Cruz tells me all I need to know. *She's a fucking keeper.*

"How far away is the aqua-air-rium?" Cruz asks as I back my car out of the driveway.

"About an hour." He slumps down into his booster seat, frowning. He's been grumpy since Mama Mel and Mama K said they wouldn't be joining us. They had every intention to join us, but at the last minute decided to hang back, conveniently claiming 'something came up.'

Cruz's little pout is enough to have Ashley craning around in her seat to ask if he wants to play I-Spy.

He perks up. "Yes!"

How easily she makes my son smile is another box checked for her, because at the end of the day, he's my number one priority. Thing is, I'm pretty sure he's hers, too.

"Awesome. I'm gonna beat you this time, too!" she says, rubbing her palms together, super-villain style.

A raspy, boyish laugh bubbles out of him. "Nu-uh!"

I listen as the two go back and forth, debating all the while about reaching over and holding her hand. I know Cruz was present when asking her for a chance, but I'm still nervous. What will he think if we're affectionate in front of him only for us not to work out? Would it confuse him—or worse, hurt him?

He cackles again when he outsmarts her with his spy, and I decide to go for it. I dart my hand out and grab ahold of hers, interlacing our fingers.

"Oh!" Ashley exclaims, and I try to pull my hand back. She holds tight though. "Not you. The salon we just passed had the cutest name, that's all."

"Oh, yeah? What was it?" Right hand to the Bible, if anyone else tried to tell me about a *cute salon name*, I'd have tuned them out in two seconds flat. But with Ashley—I want all of her words, no matter how insignificant they may be.

"It was called Southern Roots—gah! I love it!"

My lips tip up in a grin at her infectious enthusiasm. Pure and good, Ashley's one of those people whose smile makes you want to smile, too. But that's just her—she makes everything brighter...*better.*

"Are we there yet?" Cruz asks, kicking his feet against the back of my seat.

"Bud, we've only been in the car for fifteen minutes."

"And?"

"That means we have forty-five to go."

They resume their game, spotting and guessing objects until eventually, Cruz falls quiet. A quick glance in my rearview mirror confirms my suspicions—he fell asleep.

CHAPTER 34
ASHLEY

It feels like I'm floating. Like I'm suspended above my body, somewhere between elation and dismay, as Colton flies down the highway toward Bay Ridge.

From the moment I woke up, something felt different. And it wasn't just the empty bed and cool sheets that had me off-kilter. No, the very air around me was charged and thick with anticipation.

I struggled all morning to pinpoint the source of my churning gut. Even when I went outside with Cruz, Mel, and Kim, my mind raced, trying to sift through the peculiar feelings weighing me. It wasn't until I opened the card from Colton that the truth hit me like a ton of bricks.

My sixth sense was trying to warn me—to prepare me—that my soulmate was ready for me. Or on his way to ready, at the very least.

Which is where the dismay comes in, because Colton Banks is as stubborn as he is sexy, and some small part of me is still a little worried that the other shoe is yet to drop.

But for now, with my hand curled into his, I'm content to enjoy our journey.

***

We pull up to the aquarium about ten minutes before the agreed-upon time, which works in our favor as it gives Cruz time to wake up and orient himself.

"005." I unbuckle and twist around in my seat. "Wake up."

I reach out and jiggle his knobby knee, and he jerks awake. "Is it shark time?"

His excitement is so great it's almost a tangible, breathing thing with a life of its own. "Yeah, bud. It's shark time."

We clamber out of the car and head to the entrance.

"Ashley!" The sound of my best friend shouting my name rises up above the din of chatter in the aquarium lobby. "Oh my God, girl!" Mallory bear-hugs me, holding me as close as her rounded belly will allow. "I have missed you, girl!"

"I've missed you, too!" I palm her stomach like it's a basketball. "And look at you!"

"I'm the size of a house."

"You're beautiful, and you're carrying two precious babies."

Mally rolls her eyes. "Still fat."

"Preg-nant." I break the word down into syllables. "Say it with me."

"Or," she moves her eyes from side-to-side, her lips

curling into a devious grin, "you could introduce me to your friends."

"Oh!" I gasp. "Yes! This is Colton." I tug him forward to meet my best friend.

"The lawyer." She eyes him skeptically, as if trying to determine his worthiness. "Mallory Kincaid, nice to meet you."

Colton shakes her hand. "You, too. I've heard a lot about you."

"And all of it was good, I'm sure. Though, I can't say the same about you."

Her candid response has Colton shaking his head. "Ash and I got off to a bit of a rocky start."

"That's putting it mildly. Now, who is this cutie?"

"005, come meet Ashley's best friend."

Cruz scampers over to us, coming to a stumbling halt by his dad's side. "I thought I was your best friend, Agent Purple."

My heart splinters at his words. "That's the really cool thing about friends, bud. There's no limit on how many you can have. You're my best friend, but Mrs. Mally is, too."

Mallory kneels down and addresses him head on instead of letting us make the introduction. "My name is Mallory. What's yours?"

"Cruz," he whispers back, clinging to the hemline of Colton's shirt.

"Oh, I love that name. It fits you perfectly. Do you know why?"

He creeps a little closer to my knockout of a friend. "Why?"

"Because only smart, strong people have a name like Cruz."

His little blond head nods. "I am smart and strong."

"I thought so." She turns her attention back to me. "Help me up?"

Once she's back on two feet, I ask her where Natalie is.

"Right here!" comes a reply from behind me. I turn in time to see a heavily pregnant Natalie waddling toward us with Tatum skipping along happily at her side. "Sorry we're late," she huffs the words, out of breath.

I glance down at my wrist, noticeably bare of a watch. "Looks like you're right on time to me." Quickly, I introduce her and Tatum to Colton and Cruz.

Natalie also appraises my soulmate, pinning her gaze on his for several moments before nodding politely.

We head to the ticket counter, where Colton insists on covering everyone's entry—a move that undoubtedly earns him serious bonus points with my friends.

As we head into the first exhibit, Colton reaches for my hand again. The butterflies in my belly take flight at his public display of affection, flapping their wings in time to the racing beat of my heart.

He never once lets me go as the six of us move from room to room, and while each tank is more colorful and exciting than the last, Cruz seems far more interested in a certain precocious, blonde-haired little girl than he is in the fish.

About halfway through, I notice Cruz and Tatum are holding hands as well. I shoot my little Casanova a questioning look, but he merely tips his chin to where his daddy is holding my hand. *Touché, Cruz, touché.*

At each placard, Tatum reads the words to him, telling him about all of the species and varieties housed behind the thick walls of glass.

We spend extra time in the shark tunnel, letting Cruz get his fill of the massive predators.

As the magnificent beasts swim overhead, Colton wraps his arms around me from behind, resting his head on my shoulder. His eagerness to touch me so casually in front of my friends feels like a dream.

Oh, no—it this a dream?

I pinch my inner elbow. "Ouch." *Nope, not a dream.*

"You okay?" he asks, moving my braid away from my neck so he can discreetly pepper the exposed area with kisses.

I shiver beneath the feel of his lips, my breaths coming rapidly enough to fog the glass of the tank in front of me.

"Mm-hmm. Totally fine."

He moves his lips back to my ear. "You're lying."

I shake my head, insisting to him I'm not lying.

He goes to argue, but Cruz cuts him off. "Daddy," the little boy whines, "stop hogging Agent Purple so we can go see the octopus!"

I can't help but laugh at his perception of things. He seems to be taking the small developments between Colton and me in stride, but only time will tell how he really feels.

We're all disappointed when we get to the octopus's tank, as it's closed for maintenance. Cruz looks utterly heartbroken, but a hug from Tatum seems to cure his blues.

At the end, we hit up the gift shop, snagging a few mementos to remember our trip—a magnet for me, an octopus shirt for Cruz.

"Y'all wanna come to the café for a late lunch?" Natalie asks, looking and sounding a little tired.

"My daddy's café is the best ever!" Tatum announces proudly.

"The best?" Colton asks.

"The. Best." The sassy little girl cuts her eyes at him.

"Well, we better try it then."

His easy manner with kids is mind-blowing to me. For being one of the most uptight men I've ever met, he relates to kids on an almost molecular level.

"I'll text you the address or y'all can follow me," Mallory says.

"We'll just follow you."

"Actually," she interlocks her arm with mine, "why don't you ride with me? You know, so we can catch up a little more."

I turn to Colton, to find him smiling. "That sounds perfect. You two can gossip, and Cruz and I can have some guy time."

Mallory and I turn to walk away, but Colton stops me. "You're going to leave without saying bye?"

"I'll see you in—" Colton silences me with a hard press of his lips.

I freeze at first—*oh my glob, he is kissing me in front of freaking everyone*—but he gently coaxes my lips open. He slips his tongue inside, stroking it against mine in a sensual caress before pulling back leaving me dazed.

"See you in a few, Ash." He goes in for one more chaste kiss. "Be careful with my girl," he tells Mallory.

"Yeah, Mrs. Mally. Be careful with *our* girl."

Tears sting the back of my eyes; the combination of Colton's public claiming and Cruz's easy acceptance is almost too much for me to bear.

"I promise I'll be careful. Cross my heart."

CHAPTER 35
COLTON

s expected, Cruz's questions start as soon as we're alone in the car.

"Is Ashley your girlfriend? Do you love her? You kissed her, so that means you love her. Oh! If you love her, you can marry her! Then she can be my stepmom, right? Married people can have babies, can't they? Are y'all gonna give me a sister? I think I might want one, because Tatum's pretty cool. Are all girls cool like her and Agent Purple?"

"Cruz, bud." I'm barely suppressing my laughter. "Slow down."

"But I wanna know everything!" he whines.

"How about one thing at a time?"

He ponders my offer. "Fine."

"Okay, answer to question one—yes, Ashley is my… girlfriend." The way my tongue wraps around the word feels foreign to me. But at the same time, it feels right. Weirdly fucking right. "How do you feel about that?"

"Like it was…" He stops and scratches his head. "What did Gramma Mel say…oh! A long time coming."

"She said that?"

"Uh huh."

"What else did she say?"

"I'm asking the questions, Daddy."

"True, true. Next question then?"

"Do you love her?"

I open my mouth to answer him, only to promptly snap it closed. *Do I love Ashley?* Talk about a loaded question. There are definitely things about her I love. The way she cares for Cruz as if he were her own, for instance. Or the way she lives her life to the fullest and how she made a life for herself. I love her fire, her drive, and her sassy-ass mouth sure doesn't hurt either. Does loving parts of her mean I love her?

I'm at a loss on how to answer my son, my mind racing with ways to explain myself.

"It's okay, Daddy. I love her a whole bunch, and my love can be enough for both of us until you're ready to love her, too."

Unfamiliar emotion clogs my throat as I try to process his words. For only five, the kid sure is wise— probably more so than me, when it comes to matters of the heart.

"Thanks, bud. I-I appreciate that."

I catch his toothy grin in the rearview mirror. "I guess my other questions gotta wait until you love her, huh?"

I flip my blinker on and turn into Bayside Café's parking lot. "Probably so."

"Okay," he sighs, "but, Daddy?"

"Yeah?"

"Can you maybe hurry?"

ME

I miss you.

ASHLEY

I figured you'd need a break from me
after so many days together.

ME

Ashley. What I *need* is to taste your
lips. To feel your skin. To hear you say
my name as you climax.

ASHLEY

Whoa! Detour into dirty texting!

ME

It's been three days since I've seen you.

ASHLEY

I'll be home tonight and you'll see me
when you drop Cruz off tomorrow
morning.

ME

I want to see you now. It hardly seems
fair that you had to leave the second we
came home from Dogwood.

ASHLEY

If it helps, I miss you, too.

ME

Doesn't help at all.

ASHLEY

Sorry! I gotta get going if I want to make
good time on the drive home!

I meant what I said—about it not being fair. We arrived home Thursday night only for her to leave Friday morning to head down to the Florida Keys for a destination wedding.

What makes it even worse—I can't stop asking myself Cruz's question.

Do I love her?

Or am I projecting my feelings in her absence? Is going from being with her full-throttle to cold turkey amping up my desire?

I want her here. And I don't mean in Cottonwood. I want her *here.* By my side, in my house, in my bed. I meant it when I told her I wanted to explore this thing between us, and the thought of her being in my life and me not being able to touch her…kiss her…taste her—frankly, it's unacceptable.

But does that mean I love her?

I've admitted to loving things about her, but did Aristotle get it right when he said, *"The whole is more than the sum of its parts"*?

Is it Ashley that I love? Or just aspects of her?

The answer is about as clear as mud.

CHAPTER 36
ASHLEY

I raise my fist and knock, regretting it instantly. This seemed like such a good idea at the time, but now—

I'm not so sure. The words *I miss you* doesn't necessarily translate to *please show up at my house in lingerie in the middle of the night.*

And yet, here I am, doing just that.

I'm on the verge of turning and fleeing back to the safety of my car when the front door flies open, giving way to a spitting mad and adorably sleep-rumpled Colton. *Though, the anger definitely eclipses the cuteness.*

"What in the hell do you want?" he roars.

I squeak, holding my hands up in surrender as I back away from the enraged male. *So much for him missing me. My heart climbs to my throat with the thought. Maybe the shine of us wore off now that we're back in the real world. Maybe he only wants us to have a sexual fling.*

"Ashley?" He rubs his eyes and squints at me. "What are you doing here at one in the morning?"

"Nothing. It's...I-I'll go. Sorry to—"

"The only place you'll be going is my bed." He

reaches out and grabs me by the sash of my kimono and pulls me into him. I don't get another word out before his lips descend hungrily on mine.

His kiss is bruising—hard and urgent—as he infuses it with everything he isn't saying. *I missed you. I'm glad you're here. Don't go.*

Right as I expect him to deepen our kiss, he pulls away. Much to my chagrin, I whimper at the loss of contact, my needy lips following his retreat.

The sexiest of grins lights his face. "Let's take this inside, and maybe you can show me what's under this little number."

I allow him to tug me over the threshold, down the hall, and to his room. He doesn't give me a chance to take it in before he picks me up and tosses me onto the center of his enormous bed.

"You're not mad I'm here?" I ask, propping myself up on my elbows in what I hope is a sexy pose.

He shakes his head, licking his lips.

"Are you sure? Because you seemed a little...Hulk-y."

"The last time someone knocked on my door in the middle of the night it was Kelsey."

"Oh."

"Yeah, oh." He rakes his eyes over me. "But I don't want to talk about her."

"What do you want to talk about?"

His gaze darkens. "I don't want to talk at all."

Sitting up, I reach for the tie to my kimono but Colton knocks my hands out of the way.

"You can't show up here, wrapped up all pretty like a present, and then deny me unwrapping you."

My breaths saw in and out of my lungs as he tugs his

solid white T-shirt off singlehandedly, leaving him in only a pair of gray sweats. They sit low enough on his trim hips that I know he isn't wearing anything beneath them.

"Lay down and spread your legs, Ashley."

Any other day, I'd challenge him, goad him into making me, but right now I'm far too desperate for his touch. I do as he says, scooting back and laying my head on his pillow. I draw my legs up, allowing them to fall open with my knees bent and my feet planted on the mattress.

"Did you miss me, Ashley?" He reaches out for the tail end of the tie, undoing the knot in a single tug.

I moan softly and nod.

He joins me on the bed, positioning himself on his knees between my parted thighs. "You missed me so much you came here? In the middle of the night?"

"Yes, Colton." My words are nothing more than a harsh whisper as desire robs me of my voice.

"You're aching for me, aren't you?" He rubs his strong hands up my legs, from ankle to thigh. "You want me to fill this pretty pink pussy of yours and make you feel good?"

I don't know what game he's playing, but damn if I don't love it.

"Please," I whimper. My skin is flushed yet I'm chilled to the bone. I shift my hips, trying to find friction to relieve the need pounding through me. "Please touch me."

"In due time."

His voice is firm where mine is reedy. I'm a writhing mess, while he's the picture of control. We're polar opposites. And yet, perfect for one another.

He parts the sides of my kimono, sucking in a sharp breath at the sight of my body wrapped in nothing but an ivory lace thong. "You're so goddamn gorgeous."

"I need you." My voice sounds crazed, even to me. And the sexy jackass looming over me merely grins.

"You have me."

I shake my head.

"You do."

"I need you inside of me."

With those six words, Colton's control snaps. With a hungry growl, he yanks my thong down my legs, tossing the scrap of material over his shoulder before pushing his sweats down his hips.

He leans down and licks a long line up my center, but I stop him from taking it further. "No foreplay. Just fuck me."

"That mouth of yours," he murmurs as he grabs a condom from his nightstand. In the span of a single inhale, he has the thin latex barrier rolled down. He rubs the head of his dick against my slit before driving into me with one hard push.

And as I exhale, I swear, I can feel our souls collide.

"You feel so good. So tight." His face almost looks pained. "Fuck. I'm not gonna last, Ash."

He shoves his right hand between our pleasure-slicked bodies and rubs my clit in time with his thrusts.

"Yes." I hiss the word, wrapping my legs around his waist and burying my fingers in his hair, pulling him down until his lips meet mine. "Harder."

With every erotic roll of his hips, every thrust, every groan and moan, I feel our souls intertwining.

This is so much more than just sex. It's more than two people coming together. It's a fucking claiming, and as he uses his body to make me absolutely fall apart, I've never felt more whole.

Once we both recover from our climaxes, he pulls back and shoots me a cocky wink. "Told you you'd beg for it."

"You're lucky I'm too orgasmed out to think of a good comeback."

"Damn right I'm lucky." Colton pulls out and rolls off of me; my body instantly misses his welcome weight. "Come on," he says.

I stand on jelly legs and allow him to guide me toward his en suite.

The bathroom is the picture of modern luxury, with heated tile flooring, a shower big enough for five, and a soaker tub fit for royalty. Colton turns away from me to start the shower.

He's only turned away for a minute, but in those sixty seconds, doubt worms its way in.

Will he still want to be with me now that he's had me?

"What are we doing?" I ask.

"Taking a shower," he says, the *duh* implied. He steps under one of the dual shower heads, leaving the other free for me. Reluctantly, I join him. At least here, beneath the scalding spray, if he cuts me loose, the water will hide my tears.

"No. Us. What are *we* doing?"

Colton grabs his loofah and lathers up, running the sudsy sponge all over his toned body as he weighs my words.

Like the lawyer he is, he answers with a question of his own. "What do you want us to be doing?"

"I want…" I wrap my arms around myself, trying to gather my words. After a long few seconds, I decide to go for broke and lay it all out for him. "I want to be with you—in a monogamous and committed relationship. I see us having a future together—or at least the potential to. If I'm being honest, I can see myself falling in love with you."

That last bit is only partially true; I've pretty much loved Colton from the start. Even when he was awful to me, a small ember of love burned deep within me. The more time we've spent together, the larger the flame has grown. It's pretty much a freaking inferno at this point, but he doesn't need to know that.

My confession is met with stony silence.

I guess that's that.

I turn to exit the shower, but Colton blocks me. "Where are you going?"

"Home." I'm proud when my voice comes out solid.

"Why on earth would you do that?"

I whip around to face him, damn near slipping and breaking my neck.

"Easy," he says, pinning my body to his in an effort to keep me upright. "What's wrong, Ash?"

"Are you kidding me? I just poured my soul out to you, and you can't even be bothered to say anything."

"Excuse me if I didn't want to say I love you for the first time in the goddamn shower!"

I go slack in his arms, making him have to catch me all over again. "You l-love me?"

He nods, brushing his nose against my temple. "I do."

"Since when?"

"It took me a while to figure it out. Honestly, it's been on my mind for a while, but hearing you lay out your feelings just now—it kind of smacked me in the face. I love you, Ash."

"I love you, too," I murmur, happy tears blurring my vision.

Colton proceeds to wash my hair and body before wrapping me in a fluffy towel. Once dry, he pulls his previously discarded shirt over my head and tucks me into his bed. The last thing I remember before falling asleep is him whispering for me to have sweet dreams and pressing a tender kiss to my forehead before curling himself around me.

CHAPTER 37
COLTON

"Daddy." Small hands push into my chest as a weight settles on me. "Daddy! Wake up."

"Five more minutes, Cruz," I mumble sleepily. The kid definitely takes after me with his early rising, but something about this morning has me wanting to sleep in. My bed seems comfier than usual—even with my five-year-old sitting on top of me.

"Daddy! When did Agent Purple get here?"

My eyes fly open and I jack-knife up into a seated position so quickly Cruz nearly falls off the bed.

Sure enough, my purple-haired beauty is sleeping soundly beside me. Which means...*last night wasn't a dream.*

"What do you mean 'it wasn't a dream?'" Cruz asks. *Guess I said that out loud then.*

"Um. I..."

"Did you dream Ashley came here to be my mommy? Because I dream that sometimes, too." His blue eyes, so similar to my own, widen. "Is that why she's here?"

"Shh, bud." I raise my index finger to my lips. "Let's not wake up her just yet."

"But, Daddy!"

"Why don't we go make breakfast and we can talk?"

"Cheesy egg sandwiches?"

"Deal."

Cruz scrambles off of me and darts off down the hall. I stretch and give Ashley one last lingering look before following after him.

I find my little guy in the kitchen, dragging a barstool toward the fridge. "What are you doing?" I ask, stopping him in his tracks.

"Making Ashley breakfast. You said we could."

I can't help but smile at Cruz's ever-growing boldness. It's truly a testament to what stability and love can do for a kid.

"How about we make it together? I'll get the eggs and you can grab the bread?"

"Okay."

I start a pot of coffee while he gets the bread from the pantry and then the two of us start on breakfast, working in a comfortable semi-silence, aside from me offering explanations and instructions. I know Cruz has questions for me, but I wait; he'll ask them when he's ready.

Which just so happens to be after we finish our second sandwich.

"Ashley spent the night? Like a sleepover?"

"She did. How do you feel about that?"

He taps his little index finger to his chin. "When Mommy used to have her boyfriends spend the night, I didn't like it. They maked me hide and yelled a lot."

He pauses, and my drive to hunt Kelsey down reignites with a vengeance.

"But Ashley is nice to me. She smiles and plays with me and has never yelled at me, not once ever!"

"Does that mean you're okay with her sleeping over?"

"Can she do it all the time? Can she sleep with me sometimes? Or can I sleep with both of you?"

He hits me with his puppy dog eyes, and I almost say yes to all of it. Thankfully, I manage to rein it in. "I can't really answer you there, bud. Ashley has her own house, you know?"

"But we could share ours! It's big enough, right? We could even give her a bedroom!"

I stifle a laugh at his innocence and plate the third sandwich. "The thing is, bud, when two adults love each other, they want to share the same bed."

Cruz nearly reaches the ceiling he jumps so high. "You love her? I knew it! Daddy loves Ashley! Daddy loves Ashley!" He shakes his little booty as he sings his song.

"Yes, I do. I love her."

"Does that mean she can be my new mommy? Like in my dreams?"

Jesus, this kid might as well just carve up my heart.

"I don't know. This thing—our relationship—is still new."

"So?" he asks impatiently. "New things are the best."

"Why don't we take this one day at a time and see what happens?"

He pouts, but I hold firm. The last thing I want to do is get his hopes up. *I probably should've taken measures to ensure he didn't catch her in my bed, but...hindsight's twenty-twenty.*

"Fine. But I get to bring her breakfast to her."

"Sounds like a deal."

I arrange two trays—one with Ashley's sandwich, along with a single flower stem in a narrow vase, and another with mine and Cruz's food, along with a carafe of coffee, a pitcher of cream, and a juice box.

With a little help, Cruz grips his tray with both hands, and together we head down the hall back to my bedroom.

Ashley is still sleeping peacefully, curled on her side with her hands tucked beneath the pillow.

"She looks like an angel, Daddy. Our angel."

My eyes bounce from my son to the woman we both love so much. Her presence in our lives has done wonders. Maybe the kid is on to something—maybe she is an angel. A purple-haired, sexy-as-sin angel.

I help Cruz deposit his tray on her—I mean the spare—nightstand, and then place my tray down onto mine.

"Ashley?" Cruz says her name softly as he reaches for her. "Agent Purple, it's time for breakfast."

She blinks herself awake, looking positively disoriented. She sits up, looks at us, wipes at her eyes, and looks again. "Oh my," she says, her voice brimming with quiet disbelief.

"I thought the same thing when I woke up," I tell her, so she knows she's not alone in how she feels.

Oblivious to the moment, Cruz crawls up onto the bed next to her. "Good morning, Ashley. We made you breakfast, and Daddy made coffee."

She smiles at him the way a mother would her child. "Is that what smells so good?"

He nods. "Uh huh. I helped Daddy make cheesy egg sandwiches."

"And you brought it to me? Here, in bed?"

"Mm-hmm." He lays his head on her shoulder.

"That's so very sweet. Thank you."

I join them in the bed and distribute our food and drink. "Oh, this is delicious," Ashley says around a big bite. "A girl could get used to this kind of thing."

Cruz preens like a damn peacock under her praise. "If you stay, I'll make Daddy bring you breakfast in bed every single day!"

Her brows dip. "If I stay?"

Oh, Lord, here we go. Probably should have told him to keep our conversation between us.

"Yeah! Daddy said he loves you, and that when grownups love each other they share a bed. And since you're in love and all, you can marry Daddy and be my stepmom! It's perfect!"

A million different emotions play out across her face. I worry for a split-second she's going to crush my son, but like always—Ashley says the exact right thing.

"Your daddy is right. I do love him, very much. And you, too. But relationships take time and work and patience. Do you think you can be patient while your daddy and I figure things out?"

"Do I have to?" he asks with a small pout.

Ashley moves her dishes back to her nightstand and wraps Cruz up in a hug. "Please?"

"Fine." He gives her a long-suffering sigh far beyond his five years. "Only because you said the magic word, though."

Eventually Cruz grows bored of our 'boring grownup talk' and retreats to his bedroom to play. The second she hears his delighted squeal at whatever toy he's playing with, Ashley starts in with the questions.

"Colton, what…what are we doing?"

She worries her bottom lip between her teeth while nervously balling the sheets in her hands.

"What do you mean?" I know exactly what she means, but I want to see where her head's at with the whole thing.

"Are we dating or are we just fucking?"

Straight up, her words burn. At the same time, I get it. I've run so hot and cold with her it's probably pretty damn hard for her to get her footing. "Do fuck buddies usually say *'I love you?'*"

"All sorts of things can be said in the heat of the moment." She shrugs, trying—and failing—to look unaffected.

"Fine; you want me to spell it out, I'll spell it out." In one smooth motion, I have her pinned to the mattress, on her back, with me looming over her. "I. Love. You." Each word is punctuated with a kiss. "I love you, Ashley Murphy. And I'll fucking prove it. Every day, for as long as it takes for you to believe me."

"We haven't even been on a date."

"Then let's go on one. Friday night. I know you don't have a wedding this weekend, so your ass is mine." I rub my nose against hers before going in for another kiss. "Be prepared for the best date of your life, because, Ash, I don't do anything half-assed."

She licks her lips. "Promises, promises, Mr. Banks."

CHAPTER 38
ASHLEY

"Are you excited for your date with Daddy?" Cruz asks softly, curling up next to me on the couch.

"I am." I run my fingers through his messy hair.

"And you're sure I can't come, too?"

"I'm sure." He frowns. "Don't be sad, bud. You get to spend the night with Asher tonight!"

He brightens at the mention of his pint-sized pal. "Oh, yeah! Uncle West said we could make hot dogs!"

I snort out a laugh. "Uncle West is gonna buy hot dogs."

Cruz shrugs. "As long as he has ketchup…"

Ah, to be a kid again…to only worry about ketchup.

I feel horrible as soon as the thought passes. I know full and well Cruz has had to worry about far more than any kid should in his life so far.

But still—the past four days have been nothing short of pure torture, thanks to me obsessively thinking about tonight.

Date night.

I mean, sure, Cruz and I did our thing. I even made an effort to keep us extra busy. We tried three new foods this week—mangoes, starfruit, and pineapple on pizza. He loved the first two, but was absolutely horrified by the last. *Smart kid.*

We went to a movie and did more arts and crafts projects this week than most kids at summer camp. We even baked a batch of lemon bars this morning.

And yes, Colton and I have spent plenty of time together as well. Dinner every night as well as a few lunches. But he hasn't so much as kissed me since our roll in his sheets Sunday night.

I've even tried working out some of my tension with my shower head, but it's no use. I'm wound tight, on the verge of exploding.

It's half-past four when a knock sounds on my front door. "That's probably West now," I say to Cruz as I heft myself up from the couch.

Sure enough, the dark-haired man is waiting on the other side when I open the door. "Cruz!" he hollers before tipping his head my way.

"Uncle West! Is it hot dog time?"

"Damn—darn straight it is, little dude. You ready?"

Cruz's eyes ping between us, almost as if he's hesitant to leave me. "Remember, you get to hang out with Asher!"

"And," West adds, "we got a brand-new jungle gym in the backyard you boys can play on!"

"Does it have monkey bars?"

West nods. "Of course it does!"

"Ashley's been helping me. I almost got it!"

"I bet you can do it. Go grab your bag, okay?"

Cruz darts off down the hall, leaving West and me hovering in the doorway.

"Remember, he likes a nightlight and to sleep with Ollie. Also, he gets up at the crack of dawn."

West whistles. "Look at you, Mama Wolf. Take a breath. We've got this."

"I know. Truly I do. I just…I love that kid."

"He's lucky to have you. Him and his daddy."

"Thanks, but I'm the lucky one."

"Proving my point, Ashley. You're just proving my point."

I'm about to tell him to hush when Cruz bounds back into the room. He heads straight for me and wraps his arms tightly around my midsection. "I love you, Ashley."

"I love you, too, 005."

"You and Daddy have fun, okay?"

"Only if you and Asher have fun, too."

He nods solemnly. "Cross my heart."

I mimic his movements and trace an X over my heart. "If you need us—or even want us—don't hesitate to ask West or Stacia to call, okay? No matter what time, we'll talk to you or come get you. Whatever you need."

West subtly nods while Cruz crosses his arms over his chest. "I'm a big boy, Agent Purple."

I roll my lips to keep from laughing. "You are. Have fun!" With one last hug, West and Cruz head out, leaving me to rush to my bedroom to video call Mallory for outfit help.

I narrowed it down to three, but sometimes a girl needs an outside opinion.

She answers on the first ring, poised on her couch,

coffee in hand, ready to get down to business. "Let's see 'em."

A laugh bursts out of me. "Hello to you, too, Mally."

She snaps her fingers. "My ankles are swollen, my hips ache, and time's a-wasting. Let's go!"

"Slow your roll. Colton isn't picking me up until seven-thirty."

"That may be true, but I have a surprise coming at six, and you still need a shower, so…" She snaps at me again. "Let's get it in gear."

"A surprise?"

"Yes, Ashley. A dang surprise. Now, show. Me. The. Clothes."

"Fine, fine." I turn and grab the three hangers from where I left them on my bed. I show her the outfits, one by one.

"The white one, for freaking sure."

"You think?"

She looks at me like I'm dumb. "Literally said *for freaking sure.*"

"Okay, okay!" I hold my hands up in surrender. "Love you big, Mally."

"Love you bigger—now go shower!"

***

An hour later, I'm wrapped in my robe, scrubbed, shaved, and moisturized within an inch of my life. My hair is blown out and set into deep waves, looking shinier than ever thanks to my latest Insta-ad impulse purchase. All that's left is for me to slather my face with some makeup and to get dressed. There's nothing like a good book to calm my nerves. I trot into my bedroom to snag my Kindle when a knock at my front door has me course correcting.

"I swear, he better not be early," I mutter to myself, holding my robe tight with one hand and swinging the door open with the other.

"Stacia?"

Her red slicked lips tilt up in a devious grin at my confusion. "Can I come in?"

"Um, sure." I step aside to let her in. "But why?"

She wiggles her wrist, bringing my attention to the substantial makeup case she's carrying. "Your girl Mallory sent me."

"That freaking sneaky sneaker!"

"C'mon, girl, let's get your face painted fifty shades of sexy."

I lead Stacia back to my bedroom to set up in front of my vanity. I grab my foundation and moisturizer while she sets up, then sit down and let her do her thing.

Thirty minutes later, Stacia has me looking red carpet ready. My face is highlighted and contoured to dewy perfection, and my lips are a deep fuchsia color that I never would've chosen for myself.

"Ah! You're a total babe! Now let me snap a few pics."

She grabs a few from various angles before packing her stuff up.

"Hey, actually, would you mind sticking around long enough for me to get dressed? I want to send a pic to Mallory and can't selfie for shit."

"Sure, go get dressed."

I grab my clothes and scurry into the bathroom to change, donning a matching nude-colored lace bra and panty set beneath my white strappy shift dress, topping the look off with a pair of tall, lilac heels.

Stacia gives a loud catcall when I step back into the bedroom. "Girl! Colton's tongue is gonna *wag* when he sees you."

"Not going to lie, I'm excited to see his reaction."

"I wouldn't be shocked if he sprung some wood the second you open the door." She shrugs. "I'm just saying. Now, you have fun and know that Cruz is in good hands."

She takes a few pics on my phone before taking off.

Now, all that's left to do is wait.

Read and wait and try not to obsess over how our first date will go. *Gah! Who has their first date after saying 'I love you?' Talk about a curved path!*

CHAPTER 39
COLTON

knock on Ashley's door at 7:30 sharp. Waiting nearly killed me. After checking the clock for the third time in a fifteen-minute span, I gave up and decided to go for a drive to calm my nerves.

Nerves. How fucking ridiculous. I know how Ashley sounds when she comes, the way she tastes—and yet I'm nervous about taking her to dinner.

My tension eases when she answers the door looking like pure temptation dressed in white. "My God, you look good enough to eat."

She struts up to me and wraps her fingers around my lapel—just like she did at West's wedding—and smiles. "You're not too bad yourself, Mr. Banks."

Desire pulses through me, stronger than ever, but I stuff it down. Now's not the time for that—we have to have dinner before I get my dessert.

"Are you ready?"

"For you? Always."

I offer her my hand, which she readily accepts, and guide her to my car. The drive passes in a comfortable silence, the kind that comes with familiarity and content-ment—something I certainly never imagined I'd find with the woman next to me. Yet I'm so damn glad I did. I'm so incredibly thankful she never gave up on me.

Dinner passes in a blur of good food and even better conversation, but it's not until dessert that the heavier topics hit.

"Where do you see us going?" Ashley asks, dragging her spoon through the raspberry sauce on the plate.

As she brings it to her mouth and sucks it off, my first thought is *my room*. But I know she wants a serious answer. "Honestly—and please don't let this scare you off—but I see us going the distance. It feels like, I don't know, like we were meant to be here or something. A little more honesty? I feel crazy saying that; that we're meant to be here. Crazy or not, I believe it. You bring out the best in me and you're a godsend for my son. We both love you and I can see…I can see us going all the way."

By the time I finish, my cheeks are undoubtedly pink and my anxiety over her reply churns within me like a raging sea.

I'm so lost in my worry, I jump when Ashley reaches over, placing her hand on mine. She curls her fingers over the top of my hand and offers me a soft smile.

"I feel the same way. The way we did things was backward and unorthodox and yet, so totally us. You challenge me and make me feel more alive than ever. I love you—and your son—Colton Banks."

The feeling of relief her words brings is like having the weight of the world lifted from my shoulders. I'm not so stupid as to think we won't have problems going forward, but I think that, together, we can work through whatever life throws our way.

After signing the check, my hand rests on the small of her back as I walk us back to my car. Ashley's all shy smiles and lip bites, and me…I'm desperate to know what's on her mind.

"What's going on in that pretty little head of yours?" I ask as I pull away from the curb.

She swings her head my way, her heated gaze raking over me like hot coals. "How utterly devastating you look in your suit."

"You like it?"

"I do. It reminds me of when we met—I thought you were so incredibly handsome. You know, until you spoke."

I laugh lightly. "I was a bit of an ass, huh?"

"That's putting it mildly. But now you're mine." She moves her hand to rest on my arm. My fingers flex on the gear shifter as she caresses my forearm with a featherlight touch.

She gently scrapes her nails over the top of my hand, and I groan. I don't think the little temptress has any idea just how much she affects me. Especially after a week of nothing more than small kisses and even smaller touches.

I have no one to blame but myself—I told her I wanted to wine her and dine her before getting her in my bed again. Cheeky little thing even tried getting me into *her* bed on the grounds that it wasn't mine.

But I stood firm. I don't want to risk her thinking this is purely physical. Sure, she elicits a response from me unlike any other, but it's because of the *more* between us.

And with our meal done, I'm ready to get her home and have my fill of her. Double helpings, if possible.

The feeling of Ashley's hand dropping to my thigh

pulls me from thoughts of devouring what's between hers.

"Thank you for such a wonderful evening," she says, her voice all sex.

I shoot her a brief smile before returning my eyes to the road. "I'm glad you enjoyed yourself."

"I think I'd enjoy just about anything with you." She walks her fingers across my leg until her hand rests on the zipper of my slacks.

"What are you doing?" I ask, my grip on the steering wheel going white knuckled as she rubs her palm over my hardening cock.

"Dinner's over," she says, her nimble fingers tugging down the zipper as she frees me from the confines of my pants. "Dinner's over, and I want my dessert."

She leans over the console and takes me between her lips. I damn near run us off the road at the feel of her hot, wet mouth. Ashley sucks me hard before withdrawing with an audible pop.

"Fuuuuuck," I moan, my right hand moving from the gear shift to the back of her head.

Her eyes roll my way, and a self-satisfied smile lines her lips. *Dirty girl is loving this—and, oh my God, so am I.*

With great effort, I keep us in our lane and maintain the speed limit as she resumes sucking me. Her head bobs in a languid, steady tempo as she pumps my base at the same rhythm. A little moan leaves her lips with every stroke.

By the time my condo is in sight, my breathing is labored and pleasure is dancing over my skin like electricity. The muscles in my legs tense as I guide the car into my parking spot, throwing the car into park. I can't hold back any longer.

"Ashley." I run my fingers through her hair, making her moan and squirm in her seat. "Ash." I say her name again, but it's no use. She's a woman on a mission, and her mission is to wreck me with those pouty lips of hers.

Unable to hold back a second longer, I explode in her mouth. "Fuck, Ash. That was…" My words fail me. "In-*fucking*-credible."

Ashley pulls off of me and holds up her index finger, signaling me to wait. She turns away from me, pops open the passenger side door, and spits.

"Much better." She unbuckles and turns back to me. "Let's finish this inside?"

I tuck myself back into my slacks. "Yes, please."

Together, hand-in-hand, we fly to my condo. The second we're inside, I have her pinned against the door with my lips on hers. I kiss and touch her the way I've wanted to all week.

My hands roam and explore as she trembles beneath my touch. "Goddamn, I'm a lucky man," I murmur against her neck as she wraps her legs around my waist.

"I need you to fuck me." She pushes me away from her and sets off down the hall, stripping out of her dress and heels as she goes.

"With pleasure," I growl, following behind her.

By the time I catch up, she stands at the foot of my bed wearing nothing but flesh-colored lace.

"You're a goddess," I tell her, falling to my knees at her feet. "Divine. Meant to be worshiped."

"If I'm a goddess, you're a god."

"Then we can worship each other." I run my thumb over the seam of her panties, feeling her dampness even through the fabric, before pulling them down.

She braces her hands on my shoulders and steps out

of them. Unable to help myself, I lean in for a taste of her arousal. Sweet and tangy and so very Ashley.

Her fingers thread through my hair as I flick my tongue against her swollen clit. "Colt—" She breaks off in a moan. "As-as good as this feels, I need to feel you inside of me."

My body is already on fire for her, but those words— they're a match.

With one last lick, I rise to my feet. "Watch me," I tell her as I shrug out of my coat, tossing it God-knows-where. "You're meant for me, Ashley." I pop the buttons to my shirt, never taking my eyes off of her.

She rubs her thighs together as her chest heaves.

"You're mine." I do away with my belt and unfasten my pants. "Completely and irrevocably"—I shove my pants and boxers down, kicking them away— "mine."

"And you're mine, too?" she asks, a hint of vulnerability creeps into her tone.

"Solely yours, Ashley, for as long as you'll have me."

She reaches behind her and unhooks the clasp to her bra. It falls away, leaving us both deliciously naked. "Forever," she whispers. "I'll have you forever."

I press my lips to hers, sealing her vow with a searing kiss. We fall to the bed as we hungrily taste one another's lips. However, the position we land in—her on top of me—gives me an idea. "Ride me, Ashley."

She nods, nibbling on her lip.

I sheath my dick in a condom and she straddles me, sinking down onto me with a breathy moan.

She rocks against me a few times before circling her hips in slow, controlled movements meant to drive me insane.

"You feel so good," she whimpers, her nails digging into my chest, hard enough to mark me.

A sheen of sweat covers both of us as she steadily rolls her hips, giving as much pleasure as she takes.

Lifetimes pass as she moves on me—and yet, all too soon, that telltale tingle starts in my balls, telling me I'm close.

Not wanting to finish without her, I pull her in for a kiss. The arch of her back pulls me deeper into her, allowing me to hit that sweet spot with every downward rotation.

I pepper kisses down her jaw and neck. "Rub your clit, Ash. Show me how good you feel."

Her hand snakes between us, and while I can't see her actions, I feel them in the way she tightens and spasms around me.

"Oh-oh, shit, yes!" Her movements turn frantic as she chases her release. "Colton!" She screams my name as we both detonate, falling over the edge together, perfectly in sync.

Once I'm recovered from the force of my orgasm, I flip us, my semi-hard cock slipping from her warmth. I make quick work of disposing of the condom, tying it off and tossing it in the wastebasket by my bed.

Ashley, my beautiful tempting goddess, is nearly comatose with pleasure. "Colton," she sleepily murmurs my name as she reaches for me.

"Yes?"

"I love you."

I pepper her supple skin with kisses, dotting them all along her neck, shoulders, and chest. "I love you, too, Ash. More than words can express."

"I don't need your words, Colton." She nuzzles her face into the crook of my neck.

Her declaration stops me in my tracks. "What do you mean?" I fall to my back, and she immediately burrows into my side, as if the potential loss of contact is too much for her to bear.

"I don't need your words when you've given me your actions." She tangles her legs with mine and throws her arm over my chest. She yawns and smiles up at me. "Don't get me wrong, it's nice to hear, but you show me day in and day out exactly how much you love me."

I trail my fingers up and down her back as her breathing evens out and sleep claims her, vowing here and now to continue showing her day in and day out exactly how much I love her.

EPILOGUE – ASHLEY

"Mmm," my husband says as he kisses up and down my neck. "Merry Christmas, Ashley."

I arch my back, pressing my ass into his morning wood. "Happy Anniversary," I counter.

"That, too." Colton shoves a hand into my silk sleep shorts, his fingers parting my folds to dip inside me. "Already so wet for me."

"You think we have time before—"

"Mommy! Daddy! Wake up!"

Colton laughs as he withdraws his hands from my shorts. We both sit up and straighten our clothes just in time for Cruz to bound into our bedroom.

"Santa came!" Cruz crawls up onto the bed, bouncing on the space between us, excited as—well, a kid at Christmas.

"Did he?" my husband asks, his voice still thick with unsated desire.

"He did, Daddy! He did! There are so many presents! Get up!"

He climbs on top of me to reach for the baby monitor

on my nightstand. "Camilla! Wake up, sister! We have presents!" He speaks into the one-way radio like it's a walkie-talkie.

"She can't hear you, bud."

Cruz pouts.

Colton snorts out a laugh. "Why don't we go wake her up together, bud?"

"Yes! Can I hold her?"

"Once we're all sitting down, you can."

"But I'm big!" Cruz insists.

"You are," I tell him, ruffling his shaggy blond hair. "But Camilla is so very small. She's fragile."

"Okay, Mommy," Cruz says, as he drags Colton down the hall to the nursery.

My heart flutters in my chest the same way it does every time he calls me that. glob love him, he asked if he could call me mom the second Kelsey signed over her rights to Cruz, which just so happened to be on our first Christmas together. Talk about an unbeatable gift. Colton had the paperwork filed and a petition for me to adopt prepped and ready to go the very next day.

For our second Christmas, Colton and I eloped.

This year—our third Christmas—we were given the ultimate gift in the form of the sweet baby girl sleeping in the nursery down the hall.

Camilla is two months old and absolute perfection. It's crazy how well our sweet baby girl fits into our family dynamic. She's only been with us a week, but in those short seven days, she's cemented herself into our hearts with her gummy baby smiles, sweet coos, and tenacious personality.

Seriously, who knew a baby could be tenacious?

We tried for the last year to conceive, but the

universe had other plans for us. Eventually, we decided to adopt.

I like to think that our sweet, feisty Camilla was hand-picked just for us by fate. The social worker assigned to her just so happens to be the same one who helped Colton navigate the murky legal waters of fatherhood after Cruz came to him.

She and Colton have kept in touch over the years—both for work and her checking in on our sweet boy. She knew we were looking to adopt and we were the first couple she called when looking for a placement. One look into her deep mocha eyes was all it took for us to know she was meant to be ours.

The sound of Cruz singing Christmas music to Camilla filters through the monitor, bringing a watery smile to my face. I haul myself out of my warm and cozy bed and wrap myself up in my robe before setting off in search of my family.

Have mercy, that feels so good to say.

I find my three C's gathered around the tree, with Cruz pacing circles around his pile of gifts. I join Colton on the floor, graciously accepting the steaming mug of coffee he passes my way.

"Can we open them now? Please?" Cruz uses those trademark puppy dog eyes of his.

With a grin and a twinkle in his eye, Colton tells him to go for it.

It doesn't take long for our dude to tear through his presents. With each one he unwraps, he declares it his new favorite thing—even the goofy looking sweater his grandmothers sent. He demands to wear it over his jammies and we agree—quickly snapping a pic to capture the moment.

Once his pile is complete, he moves on to Camilla's. Oblivious to the fact that his baby sister is sound asleep in her daddy's lap, he announces each gift and holds it up for her to see.

I lock eyes with my husband and smile, knowing the best is yet to come.

"Cruz, you want to help me give Daddy his big super special gift?"

"Yeah!" He leaps up and does a little happy dance. "You're gonna love it, Daddy!"

I can't help but laugh at his excitement because the kid is totally in the dark over what I have wrapped up beneath the tree. I point to a small rectangular package and Cruz darts over to it, tripping over the scooter Santa brought him, snatches up the gift, and drops it to the floor in front of Colton.

"I thought we weren't exchanging gifts," Colton says, placing Camilla in my waiting arms.

A giggle escapes me. "Right, like I don't know you broke the rules, too, and have my gifts stashed behind the couch."

The look on his face is priceless. "How do you know?"

I give him an *oh, please* sort of look. "Mr. Banks, I know you better than you know yourself."

"That you do, Ash."

"Now hush up and open my gift."

A million butterflies take flight in my belly as he cocks his head, studying me and then the gift.

I hold my breath as he runs his index finger beneath the seam of the shiny paper. He tears it away and pries the lid off of the box it was covering, pulling from it a small silver frame.

I struggle to swallow down the lump forming in my throat as he turns the frame over. He looks to me with tears in his gorgeous blue eyes.

"Is this…"

I'm nodding and smiling and crying and feeling every single emotion ever all at once. "Yes."

"You're…"

"*We're* having a baby!"

He leans over and kisses me hard on the lips. "Best Christmas ever," he whispers, resting his forehead against mine. He laughs through his nose. "Oh my God, we're having a baby."

Not one to be left out, Cruz worms his way between us. "I'm getting another baby?"

"You are," I whisper to him, happy tears dotting my lashes.

Burying his head into my chest, he sniffles. "Is this baby gonna poop, too? Because Camilla stinks bad!"

Once our laughter subsides, Colton turns to me. "Did you ever think this would be us?"

Solemnly, I nod.

"Really?"

"Absolutely. I knew from the moment we met we'd end up together."

"Get real, Ash."

I grin up at my stubborn husband. "I mean it. I knew the second I laid eyes on you that you were my soulmate. Why do you think I never gave up?"

"I thought you were crazy." He laughs. "God, I was awful to you."

"You weren't so bad." I knock my shoulder against his. "Plus, look where we ended up. This life with you—

it's worth every single ounce of heartache. *You are* worth every lump, bump, and curve, Colton Banks."

"You really knew?"

"Cross my heart," I say, drawing an 'X'.

"Damn, Ash," he murmurs, wrapping an arm around my waist, holding me close. "I'm…" he trails off.

"I know, I know." I crane my neck and press a kiss to his jaw. "You're glad I had enough good sense and faith for both of us."

He growls playfully. "Cheeky woman."

"You love it."

"Damn right, I love you. Today, forever, and always."

THE END.

BEFORE YOU GO

Sign up for Kate's mailing list and/or join her group to stay up to date with all of her bookish happenings, from sales to exclusive content.

No spam, just good books, and that's a promise!

LK'S OTHER TITLES

All of LK's titles can be read as standalones & are available with Kindle Unlimited. An * beside a title denotes it is also available in audio.

<u>Sweet Little Nothing</u> * (an enemies-to-lovers/bully romance)

<u>Dirty Little Secret</u> * (an older brother's best friend/second chance romance)

<u>Pretty Little Thing</u> * (a single mom/forced proximity/mistaken identity romance)

<u>Best Laid Plans</u> * (an older brother's best friend/secret baby romance)

<u>Best of Intentions</u> * (a friends-to-lovers/little sister's best friend romance)

<u>Best of Me</u> * (a second chance at love/forbidden twin romance)

<u>Rebel Heart</u> (an enemies-to-lovers jock/tutor rom-com)

<u>Rebel Soul</u> (an arranged baby/friends-to-lovers rom-com)

<u>Rebel Desire</u> (an unrequited soulmates/surprise single dad rom-com)

<u>Coming Up Roses</u> * (a small-town/single mom romance)

<u>An Uphill Battle</u> * (a frenemies-to-lovers romance)

<u>Weather the Storm</u> (a second chance at love romantic suspense)

<u>Come What May</u> (an age gap/single dad romance)